Book Two of The Taravale Series

EMILY FRASER

WHAT THE LAND LEAVES

What the Land Leaves

Book Two of The Taravale Series

Copyright © 2026 Emily Fraser

This is a work of fiction. Names, characters, places, and incidents are the product of the author's imagination or are used fictitiously. Any resemblance to actual persons, living or dead, or real events is coincidental.

First edition 2026

Published by Southern Ground Press, Australia

ISBN (paperback): 978-1-7645031-1-2

ISBN (ebook): 978-1-7645031-2-9

Printed in Australia

For those who stayed when leaving
would have been easier.

AUTHOR'S NOTE

What the Land Leaves is a story about consequence.

Not punishment. Not justice neatly delivered. But the quieter cost of choosing truth when silence would have been easier.

If the first book asked what we inherit, this one asks what remains after we stop pretending we can carry it all without loss.

Taravale is still fictional. The choices are not.

This is a book about visibility - about what happens when a private reckoning becomes a public one, and when love, community, and land are all tested by the same question: *What are you willing to give up to do the right thing?*

Some things burn. Some things leave. Some things survive only because they are stripped back to what is essential.

This book is for those who stand anyway. For the ones who stay honest when it costs them.

Thank you for continuing the journey with Alice.

CHAPTER ONE

The first thing Alice learned about loving someone at Taravale was that the land noticed.

It wasn't dramatic. It didn't announce itself with signs or omens or the kind of warning people liked to tell stories about later. It was more subtle than that. A hesitation. A refusal. As if the place itself had paused and decided not to make things easy anymore.

She stood at the kitchen sink, early light stretching thin and pale across the floorboards, and waited for the tap to steady. It didn't. The water sputtered, then settled into a weaker flow than it should have, the sound wrong in a way she couldn't quite explain.

Alice frowned, turned it off, and leaned her hip against the bench.

Outside, Taravale looked the same as it had every morning since she'd woken here with the sense that this place might finally hold her. Frost still clung to the low grass. The paddocks rolled out toward the ridge, grey-green and patient. The old gums stood exactly where they always had.

Nothing looked broken.

That was the problem.

She pulled on her boots and stepped out onto the verandah, the cold biting straight through the soles. The air smelled sharp, clean, honest. Fire season had officially ended weeks ago, but the country still held that dry, watchful tension it always carried beneath the surface.

Alice crossed the yard, her breath puffing white, and checked the trough by the house. The float sat lower than it should have. Not empty. Not alarming. Just... off.

"You're imagining it," she murmured, more to herself than the land.

She'd learned, over the last year, how easy it was to project feelings onto a place like this. Taravale had a way of absorbing whatever you brought with you and feeding it back until you were sure it had always been there.

Love included.

She straightened, rolled her shoulders, and scanned the paddock where the cattle clustered near the fence line. They lifted their heads as one when they saw her, a few stepping forward, curious. They looked fine. Calm. Healthy.

Still, the unease didn't lift.

Alice turned back toward the house just as the screen door creaked open behind her.

Tom stepped out, already dressed, sleeves rolled, hair still damp from the shower. He held a mug in one hand, steam curling up into the cold air. His presence settled something in her chest without her permission.

"You're up early," he said.

"So are you."

He shrugged. "Couldn't sleep."

That, too, felt new. Tom had always slept like the dead, the kind of man who trusted morning to arrive whether he was conscious for it or not. Lately, though, he'd been waking before dawn, restless in a way he never quite explained.

Alice hadn't pushed. Not yet.

"The water's odd," she said instead.

Tom frowned, immediately attentive. "How?"

"Pressure's low. Trough's dropped more than it should overnight."

He took a sip of coffee, eyes moving automatically to the tank, the lines, the lay of the land. "Could be a valve. I'll check it after breakfast."

She nodded. Sensible. Ordinary. The kind of explanation that should have been enough.

He watched her for a moment, something unreadable crossing his face. "You alright?"

"Yes," she said, too quickly. Then softened it. "Just... thinking."

He smiled faintly. "Dangerous habit."

Alice snorted despite herself and leaned into him when he stepped closer, the warmth of his body cutting through the chill. His arm came around her waist with easy familiarity, thumb resting just above her hip as if it had always belonged there.

It still startled her, how natural it felt. How quickly this had become real.

She rested her forehead against his chest, listening to the steady thump of his heart. "Do you ever get the feeling," she said slowly, "that a place can change its mind about you?"

Tom stilled.

Just for a second. Just long enough for her to notice.

"I think places are like people," he said carefully. "They don't change their minds. They just remember things you didn't know about."

She pulled back to look at him. "That's... not comforting."

"No," he agreed. "It's honest, though."

Alice studied his face, the lines she'd come to know, the steadiness she trusted. There was nothing there that said danger. Nothing that said regret.

Still, the unease lingered, like smoke after a fire you were sure was out.

"Breakfast?" he offered.

She nodded, and they went inside together.

Later, after he'd left to check the lines, Alice sat at the table with her laptop open, sorting through emails she'd been putting off. Most were routine. Feed suppliers. A neighbour asking about agistment. A council notice she almost deleted without reading.

Almost.

Notice of Review – Historical Water Allocation

She opened it, skimmed the language, the dates. It was dry. Procedural. Just a notification that certain properties within the catchment were undergoing a routine audit.

Routine, her instinct repeated, even as something colder settled beneath it.

Taravale was named.

So were properties she recognised. Families who'd been here longer than anyone remembered. Names that carried weight in the district.

She scrolled, eyes catching on a familiar surname.

Tom's.

Alice leaned back in her chair, the kitchen suddenly too quiet.

Outside, a breeze moved through the trees, lifting leaves, shifting shadows across the yard. The land went on, unchanged and indifferent.

She told herself she was overthinking it. That this was how ownership worked. How systems worked. How the world functioned when you weren't hiding from it anymore.

Still, when Tom came back inside, smelling of dust and cold air, she didn't tell him about the email right away.

She watched him instead. The way he moved through the space. The way he belonged here.

CHAPTER TWO

The thing about paperwork, Alice thought, was that it always arrived looking polite.

She read the notice again after Tom left for the back paddock, slower this time, letting each line settle. *Routine audit. Historical allocation. No immediate action required.*

Language designed to calm. Language designed to keep people from asking questions.

She closed the laptop and stood, pacing the length of the kitchen. The house was warm now, the heater ticking softly, yesterday's mugs still in the sink. Nothing in this room suggested trouble. Nothing here hinted at land disputes or inherited wrongs or anything that could reach back far enough to tangle the present.

Still, Taravale had been here longer than any of them.

Alice pulled on her jacket and walked down toward the creek line, boots crunching over frost-softened dirt. The water ran low but steady, glinting dully between the reeds. She crouched and dipped her fingers in. Cold. Clean. Ordinary.

She straightened and looked upstream.

It had taken her a long time to learn that *ordinary* didn't always mean *right*.

Later, she rang the number listed at the bottom of the notice. A woman answered, efficient and kind, the sort of voice that had learned how to deliver information without absorbing it.

"Yes, Mrs- Alice," she corrected herself automatically, still not used to the absence of a surname that tied her to someone else's history. "I'm calling about the audit notice."

"Of course," the woman said. Keyboard clicks. "Taravale, yes?"

Alice's jaw tightened. "That's right."

"It's standard," the woman continued. "We're reviewing allocations granted prior to the reforms. Some records weren't digitised properly at the time."

"And Taravale?" Alice asked. "Is there an issue?"

A pause. Barely there, but enough.

"At this stage, we're just gathering information."

Alice had learned to translate phrases like that. *At this stage* meant *we don't know yet. Gathering information* meant *someone is going to be unhappy.*

"Will we need to provide anything?" Alice asked.

"We may request access to historical infrastructure," the woman said. "Old channels. Pipes. Tanks."

Alice closed her eyes.

Infrastructure meant evidence. Evidence meant history. History, she was beginning to understand, was rarely neutral.

After she hung up, she sat at the table again and opened the laptop, pulling up old property records she'd scanned months ago and never properly read. Titles. Transfers. Notes scribbled in margins by hands long dead.

She wasn't looking for anything specific.

That, she realised, was the worst part.

By the time Tom came back in for lunch, Alice had a headache and a creeping sense that she'd stepped onto a track she couldn't leave.

"You look like you're working too hard," he said, setting bread and cheese on the counter.

"I rang the department," she replied.

He froze.

Not fully. Not obviously. Just enough.

"And?" he asked.

"They're auditing historical water allocations."

Tom nodded slowly, as if this were something he'd always known would come. "That happens."

"Yes," Alice said. "It does."

She watched him carefully now, noticing the way he avoided her eyes, the way his shoulders held tension he hadn't bothered to hide before.

"They might want access to old infrastructure," she added.

"I know."

The word landed heavy between them.

"You know," she repeated.

He exhaled, set the knife down more carefully than necessary. "Alice-"

"Don't," she said quietly. "Don't explain yet. Just tell me if I should be worried."

Tom met her gaze then, and she saw something there she hadn't before. Not fear. Not guilt.

Calculation.

"It depends," he said. "On what they find."

Alice swallowed. "And what might they find?"

He hesitated.

Just a second too long.

"Old decisions," he said finally. "Made when people thought survival justified things that wouldn't be allowed now."

"Survival for who?"

Tom didn't answer.

That night, lying beside him in the dark, Alice stared at the ceiling and listened to the familiar sounds of the house settling around them. His arm rested heavy over her waist, protective, possessive, warm.

She loved him.

That truth had settled quietly over the last weeks, unannounced and irreversible. It didn't frighten her anymore. What frightened her was the way love had a habit of blinding you to things you should be brave enough to see.

Outside, the land held its breath.

CHAPTER THREE

Alice woke before dawn with Tom's arm heavy across her waist and the weight of yesterday still lodged behind her eyes.

For a few seconds, she lay still, listening. The house breathed around them - timber ticking, pipes settling, the faint rush of water somewhere beyond the walls. The rhythm of Taravale at rest.

Tom slept deeply beside her, his face turned into her shoulder, breath warm against her skin. She traced the line of his jaw with her fingertips, slow and absent-minded, the way you touched something familiar to reassure yourself it was real.

It still surprised her how quickly he had become this.

Not a guest. Not a possibility. A presence.

She slid carefully from the bed, pulling on a jumper and stepping into the kitchen to make coffee. Outside, the sky was just beginning to pale, the paddocks blurred and soft through the window. This was her favourite time of day - when the land hadn't yet decided what it would ask of you.

The kettle clicked off.

She poured the water, waited for the grounds to bloom, and tried not to think about audits or records or the way Tom had said *I know.*

She was halfway through her mug when his arms slipped around her from behind.

"You always leave the bed cold," he murmured into her hair.

She smiled despite herself. "You steal the blankets."

"I provide body heat."

"You snore."

He huffed a laugh and tightened his grip, chin resting on her shoulder. They stood like that for a moment, quiet and domestic, the steam from their mugs fogging the window.

Alice closed her eyes.

"This," she said softly, "is dangerous."

Tom stiffened slightly. "The coffee?"

"Us."

He turned her gently, crowding her back against the bench. "You don't sound like someone who wants to stop."

She didn't. That was the problem.

"I sound like someone who knows better," she said. "And is ignoring it anyway."

His mouth curved. "That's my favourite version of you."

She should have laughed it off. Should have stepped away, finished her coffee, kept this careful.

Instead, she rose onto her toes and kissed him.

It wasn't tentative. It wasn't exploratory. It was the kind of kiss that came from days of holding back, of pretending that touch hadn't already rewired her.

Tom swore softly and lifted her onto the bench without asking, mugs abandoned, his hands firm on her hips. She wrapped her legs around him instinctively, pulling him closer, needing the contact in a way that felt almost urgent.

This wasn't about lust.

It was about reassurance. About choosing something solid in a world that had started to tilt.

They didn't rush. They didn't speak much either. Clothes were shed in stages, unhurried, as if they both understood that this moment mattered.

Later, Alice lay sprawled across the bed, sheets tangled around her legs, Tom's fingers tracing idle patterns on her skin.

"Stay," she said before she could stop herself.

He paused. "I live here."

"That's not what I mean."

He shifted, propping himself up on one elbow to look at her properly. "Alice-"

"Just… stay," she repeated. "With me. Whatever comes."

The honesty of the plea surprised them both.

Tom's expression softened, then shuttered. He leaned down and kissed her forehead instead of answering.

"I'm not going anywhere," he said.

It sounded true.

By mid-morning, Alice had pushed the doubts aside and thrown herself into work. Paperwork. Phone calls. Distractions. She was halfway through sorting fencing invoices when the ute pulled into the yard.

She glanced out, expecting Tom.

Instead, a white government vehicle idled by the gate.

Her stomach dropped.

The man who introduced himself was polite, efficient, mid-forties, sun-worn in the way of someone who spent more time on properties than in offices.

"Just a preliminary visit," he said, clipboard tucked under his arm. "We're touching base before the formal review."

"Of course," Alice said, forcing calm. "What do you need?"

"Just to walk the creek line. Note existing infrastructure."

She nodded, grabbed her hat, and led him down the slope.

They walked in silence for a while, the man stopping occasionally to jot notes, to photograph a pipe half-hidden by grass, an old concrete channel Alice had always assumed was harmless.

"This was installed when?" he asked.

"I'm not sure," she admitted. "Before my time."

He nodded. "That's often the case."

When they reached the bend in the creek, he stopped and crouched, brushing away debris to reveal something older beneath - rusted metal, deliberate, placed with intent.

Alice followed his gaze, her chest tightening.

Behind them, smoke lifted faintly from a neighbour's burn-off, the smell sharp on the air.

She thought of Tom's hesitation. Of the way the land had begun to resist.

And for the first time, Alice understood that loving him hadn't just tied her to a man.

It had tied her to everything he hadn't yet said.

CHAPTER FOUR

Alice woke before the sun.

Not because of worry - not yet - but because the land had taught her to listen for the moment when sleep stopped being useful. The house was cool, the air holding the faint smell of stone and old timber. Somewhere outside, a bird tested the morning with a single note, then waited.

Alice lay still for a moment, eyes open, letting her body decide if it was ready.

It was.

She swung her legs out of bed and pulled on clothes without turning on the light, movements learned and automatic. The floor was cold under her feet. She welcomed it. Cold sharpened things.

Outside, the paddocks were still grey, the sky undecided. Alice stepped onto the verandah with her mug and breathed in deeply.

Dry, she thought. Too dry for this early.

She walked down toward the yards, boots scuffing the ground, checking the small things first

- a gate that sometimes didn't latch properly, a trough she'd marked to keep an eye on. The work was ordinary, repetitive, and quietly reassuring.

This was what she trusted.

The trough level had dropped more than she liked. Not dramatically - not enough to alarm anyone who wasn't looking closely - but enough to register. Alice leaned over the rail, watching the water settle.

She'd learned the land's tells the way other people learned moods. Small shifts. Hesitations. Patterns that didn't quite repeat the way they should.

She made a note in the small notebook she kept tucked into her pocket.

Later, she told herself. I'll check again later.

The sun crept higher, washing the paddocks in pale gold. The gumtrees along the creek line stirred, bark peeling in soft ribbons that crunched underfoot when she crossed the bend.

Alice crouched and ran her fingers through the soil.

Dusty. Loose.

She stood and wiped her hands on her jeans, feeling the familiar tug of concern without letting it turn into panic. This was what land ownership looked like most days - quiet monitoring, steady response, no drama.

Back at the house, she leaned against the bench and drank the rest of her tea.

The kitchen felt settled now. Lived in. No longer waiting for her to prove she belonged there.

Tom's mug sat beside the sink.

Alice picked it up, rinsed it, and put it away in the cupboard without thinking too much about it. Some habits stayed. Some changed shape.

She checked the calendar pinned to the wall. Notes in her own handwriting marked days that mattered: maintenance, meetings, things she hadn't learned to forget yet.

Nothing looked urgent. That was the lie mornings liked to tell.

Alice stepped back outside and walked the boundary closest to the creek, counting posts as she went. She'd always done that - an old habit from childhood - as if numbering them kept the land anchored.

When she reached the far corner, she stopped and looked back across Taravale.

From here, the property looked peaceful. Ordered. Almost forgiving.

Alice knew better.

The land didn't forgive. It responded.

She stood there longer than she needed to, the breeze lifting the hair at the nape of her neck, the quiet stretching comfortably around her.

This, she thought, was why she stayed.

Not because it was easy. Because it was honest.

When she turned back toward the house, the sun was properly up, the day already warming. Alice adjusted her hat, squared her shoulders, and set off toward the next task without hurry.

There would be time later for whatever this day wanted from her.

For now, the land required attention.

And Alice gave it.

CHAPTER FIVE

By the time the dust from the government ute settled back onto the drive, Alice felt as though Taravale had shifted a few inches beneath her feet.

Not enough to throw her off balance.

Enough to make her aware of every step.

She stood on the verandah longer than necessary after the man left, arms folded against the chill that had nothing to do with temperature. The smell of smoke from the neighbouring burn-off still lingered faintly in the air, sharp and unsettling. It was the wrong smell at the wrong time of year, and it lodged somewhere deep in her chest.

She went inside and opened her laptop again.

The email arrived less than an hour later.

Subject: Follow-Up: Site Inspection – Taravale
Sender: Catchment Management Authority

Polite. Neutral. Precise.

Thank you for your time today. Following our preliminary site visit, we will be progressing to a formal review of historical infrastructure and associated allocations. You will be contacted shortly regarding documentation requests and access arrangements.

Alice stared at the screen until the words blurred.

Formal review.

That was the phrase that changed everything.

She forwarded the email to Tom without comment and closed the laptop, her hands shaking. She pressed them flat on the table and breathed until the tremor eased.

This was manageable, she told herself. Processes always felt bigger at the beginning. Once you knew the rules, once you understood what was being asked of you, it became just another thing to handle.

The problem was that Taravale had never been built on rules.

It had been built on decisions.

Tom came in just after lunch, boots muddy, face set in a way that told her he'd already read the email.

"They've moved fast," he said.

"Yes," Alice replied. "They tend to."

He pulled a chair out and sat heavily, elbows braced on the table. For a moment, neither of them spoke.

"How bad is it?" she asked finally.

Tom dragged a hand through his hair. "That depends on what records still exist."

"And if they don't?"

He looked at her then, really looked at her, and she felt the shift in him - the moment where he stopped shielding and started measuring what truth would cost.

"Then they'll go looking for physical evidence," he said. "Which they've already started doing."

Alice swallowed. "And what will that show?"

"That water was redirected. Quietly. Legally at the time - or close enough that no one challenged it."

"Who lost out?" she asked.

Tom hesitated. Again.

"People downstream," he said. "Families who didn't have the influence to fight it."

The words settled heavily between them.

Alice stood and crossed to the window, staring out at the paddocks she'd come to love. The land looked unchanged, indifferent to the weight it carried.

"How long have you known?" she asked.

"Since before you came," he said quietly.

She turned back to him. "And you didn't think that mattered?"

"I thought it was buried," he replied. "I thought it had already taken what it was going to take."

Alice laughed softly, without humour. "That's not how this place works."

"No," he agreed. "It isn't."

She leaned against the bench, arms folded tight around herself. "So what happens now?"

Tom exhaled slowly. "Now they trace the allocations. They interview people. They look at who benefited and who didn't."

"And Taravale?" she asked.

"Taravale will be central."

The word landed like a blow.

Alice nodded once. Twice. She was careful with her movements now, as if sudden shifts might crack something fragile inside her.

"I need to know everything," she said. "Not pieces. Not later."

Tom stood and stepped toward her. She didn't move away, but she didn't lean into him either.

"I know," he said. "I should have told you sooner."

"Yes," Alice replied. "You should have."

That night, she lay awake long after Tom's breathing evened out beside her. The house felt different now - no longer a refuge, but a structure standing on ground that might not hold.

She thought about the pipe the inspector had uncovered. About how deliberately it had been placed. How someone, years ago, had stood exactly where she had stood today and made a choice that rippled forward in ways they couldn't-or wouldn't-see.

Outside, the wind picked up, moving through the trees with a dry whisper.

Alice closed her eyes and listened.

Taravale wasn't angry.

It was patient.

CHAPTER SIX

Alice had never been sentimental about paperwork.

She respected it. Trusted it, even. Paper had rules. It told you where you stood. It didn't soften things to spare your feelings.

By mid-morning, she'd cleared the dining table and spread the contents of the old filing cabinet across it: brittle manila folders, handwritten notes, maps folded so many times the creases had worn thin. The smell of dust and age clung to her fingers.

Tom had offered to help.

She'd said no.

Not unkindly. Not accusingly. Just firmly.

"This is mine," she'd said. "I need to see it myself."

He'd accepted that with a nod she was starting to recognise as restraint.

Alice worked slowly, scanning dates, names, cross-referencing transfers and approvals. Most of it was dull. Necessary. The kind of material no one looked at unless they had to.

And then there were the gaps.

Years where the paperwork thinned. Correspondence that referenced meetings without minutes. Handwritten annotations in margins that meant nothing on their own and everything when you placed them beside something else.

She opened a leather-bound ledger she'd almost missed, tucked behind a stack of invoices from the nineties. The handwriting inside was neat, slanted slightly to the right, the ink faded but legible.

Water flow. Maintenance costs. Notes about "temporary measures."

Temporary, she'd learned, had a habit of becoming permanent when no one was watching.

Alice turned page after page, her pulse steady but intent sharpening. Dates lined up with changes she'd seen on the maps - channels added, lines redirected, approvals signed by people who no longer existed in any system she could search.

At midday, she paused and rubbed her eyes, realising she hadn't eaten. The house was quiet. Too quiet. Tom was out on the back boundary, and the absence of his presence felt deliberate now, as if both of them understood that this part required separation.

She poured herself a glass of water and drank it slowly, the irony not lost on her.

By the time she sat back down, she knew what she was looking for.

Not proof.

Pattern.

And there it was.

A series of small changes, each justifiable on its own. Each framed as necessary. Each signed off by someone who benefited from the next decision.

The ledger entries stopped abruptly in the early 2000s.

Alice flipped the page, expecting continuation.

Instead, she found a folded sheet tucked between the pages.

It was a letter.

Not official. No letterhead. Just a single page, typed, yellowed at the edges.

We can't keep pretending this is temporary. They're already asking questions. If this comes out, it won't just be the allocations they look at.

Alice's throat tightened.

There was no signature. Just initials at the bottom - two sets.

One she recognised.

Tom's family name.

She sat back slowly, the chair scraping softly against the floorboards. This wasn't just about water. This wasn't just about who had more and who had less.

This was about concealment.

Outside, the wind shifted, pushing against the side of the house. Alice stared at the letter until the words blurred, then folded it carefully and slid it back where she'd found it.

She didn't feel shocked.

She felt... clear.

That afternoon, she walked the boundary lines herself, notebook tucked under her arm. She noted infrastructure she'd never questioned before. Old concrete. Rusted fittings. The quiet logic of things that had been placed with intention and then left to become invisible.

When Tom joined her near the fence line, she didn't confront him.

Not yet.

They walked side by side, boots crunching over dry earth, the sky stretched wide and untroubled above them.

"You're quiet," he said.

"I'm thinking," she replied.

He nodded. "Me too."

That night, they made dinner together, moving around each other with the ease of habit. They ate at the table, talked about practical things - feed deliveries, repairs, a neighbour's sale - as if nothing had shifted.

But later, in bed, when Tom reached for her, Alice hesitated.

Just for a moment.

He noticed.

"What is it?" he asked softly.

She pressed her forehead to his chest, listening to the heartbeat she'd come to rely on.

"I'm not pulling away," she said. "I just need you to understand something."

"Tell me."

"If this costs Taravale," she said, "I won't lie to save it."

His breath caught.

"I won't lie to save you either."

The words hung between them, heavy and honest.

Tom's arms tightened around her. "I wouldn't ask you to."

Alice closed her eyes.

She wasn't sure that was true.

And for the first time since she'd let herself love him, she understood that the land wasn't the only thing keeping score.

CHAPTER SEVEN

Alice didn't ask the question right away.

She learned long ago that the wrong moment could turn truth defensive, brittle. So she waited. She answered emails. She let the day wear on until the light softened and the heat drained from the paddocks.

It was late afternoon when she found Tom in the machinery shed, tools spread out around him, sleeves rolled, jaw tight with concentration. He looked up when he heard her boots on concrete.

"Everything alright?" he asked.

"Yes," she said. "No."

He straightened slowly. "Which one do you want to talk about?"

Alice leaned against the workbench, the ledger tucked under her arm, the letter folded inside it like a held breath.

"When did you first know it wasn't just about water?" she asked.

Tom's expression barely changed. That was answer enough.

"Alice-"

"No," she said gently. "Just answer the question."

He exhaled through his nose and set the spanner down with care. "Before you came," he said. "Not long before."

"And you didn't think that mattered?"

"I thought it was finished," he replied. "I thought whatever damage had been done was already absorbed."

"By who?" she asked.

He closed his eyes briefly. When he opened them, the calculation was gone.

"By people who didn't have a choice," he said.

Alice nodded once. She pulled the ledger free and opened it, flipping to the page she'd marked.

"I found this," she said, handing it to him.

Tom's fingers tightened on the leather cover as he read. He didn't need long. He didn't read the letter twice.

When he looked up, his face had gone pale.

"You weren't meant to see that," he said.

"I live here," Alice replied. "That makes it mine."

He nodded. Slowly. "Yes."

She waited. Let him decide how much truth to offer.

"It started as survival," he said at last. "Drought years. Families going under. Decisions made quietly, with handshakes and promises. No one thought they were stealing. They thought they were redistributing."

"And when people noticed?"

"They were told it was temporary," he said. "That things would be made right later."

Alice's mouth tightened. "Later never comes."

"No," he agreed. "It doesn't."

She closed the ledger and tucked it back under her arm. "Was anyone hurt?"

Tom hesitated.

"That's not a question you pause on," Alice said softly.

He looked at her then, really looked, and whatever he saw there made him answer.

"A man died," he said. "Officially, it was an accident. Slipped near the channel during repairs."

Alice's stomach dropped. "Unofficially?"

"The channel shouldn't have been there."

Silence stretched between them, thick and unforgiving.

"And your family?" she asked. "Where do you sit in this?"

He swallowed. "Beneficiaries. Not architects. But we knew. We stayed quiet."

Alice closed her eyes. When she opened them again, something had settled into place.

"This is bigger than us," she said.

"Yes."

"And staying quiet now would make me complicit."

"Yes."

Tom stepped closer, reaching for her. She let him - but she didn't lean into it this time.

"I love you," she said. The words were steady. Certain. "That doesn't change because of this."

His breath hitched.

"But it doesn't excuse it either," she continued. "And I won't be protected by omission."

"I know," he said hoarsely. "That's why I didn't want you dragged into it."

She met his gaze. "You didn't drag me. You loved me. That's worse."

He let out a broken laugh. "I was hoping you wouldn't see it that way."

"I see things clearly," Alice said. "It's one of my flaws."

She stepped back, creating space between them.

"I'm going to cooperate fully," she said. "With everything. Even if it costs Taravale. Even if it costs us."

Tom nodded once, sharp and final. "Then I need to start preparing."

"For what?" she asked.

"For the possibility that the only way to keep you out of this," he said quietly, "is to remove myself from it."

The words landed like a blow.

Alice stared at him, the echo of them ringing in her ears.

"You don't get to decide that alone," she said.

Tom's jaw tightened. "I already decided something alone once. I won't do it again without telling you."

Outside, the wind rose, dry and restless, moving through the trees with the sound of something approaching.

Alice understood then that the question she'd asked had done exactly what she'd feared.

It hadn't revealed the truth.

It had set it in motion.

CHAPTER EIGHT

The first thing to change was the silence between them.

Not the comfortable kind - the kind that settles in when two people know each other well enough not to fill every gap. This was sharper. Alert. Like both of them were listening for something they couldn't yet hear.

The mail arrived mid-morning, thick and official, and Alice didn't bother opening it straight away. She left it on the hall table, face down, as if ignoring it might buy her a few more hours of normal.

It didn't.

By the time Tom came in from the yards, dust on his boots and tension riding his shoulders, the envelope had become unavoidable. He picked it up without asking, read it once, then again more slowly.

"They want interviews," he said.

Alice leaned against the bench, arms folded. "I know."

He looked at her, searching her face. "Mine first."

"Yes."

The word sat between them, final and unsoftened.

He set the envelope down and stepped closer to her. Just close enough that she could feel the warmth of him, the familiar gravity that pulled her in even now.

"You're angry," he said.

"I'm scared," she corrected. "Anger would be easier."

Tom exhaled slowly. "I hate that this is touching you."

"It already has," Alice replied. "You don't get to decide when."

Something shifted in his expression then - resignation giving way to something darker, more physical. He reached for her, hands firm at her waist, grounding.

"This isn't fair," he murmured.

"No," she agreed, tipping her head back as his mouth brushed her jaw. "But it's real."

The kiss that followed wasn't gentle.

It wasn't rushed either.

It was the kind of kiss that came from too much restraint and not enough certainty - mouths meeting with intention, bodies aligning because they already knew how. Alice felt it immediately, the way her body responded faster than her thoughts, the way wanting him cut through everything else.

Tom backed her against the bench, hands spanning her hips, thumbs pressing in like he needed to feel her there. She threaded her fingers into his shirt, tugging him closer, needing the weight of him, the proof.

This wasn't about escape.

It was about claiming something before it was taken.

They moved together through the house without speaking, hands never leaving skin, contact constant and demanding. The bedroom door barely closed before Tom had her pressed against it, forehead resting against hers as if steadying himself.

"Tell me to stop," he said quietly.

She didn't hesitate. "Don't."

They undressed each other without ceremony, without urgency born of novelty. This was familiarity sharpened by risk - every touch deliberate, every breath heavy with meaning. Alice let herself feel it all: the way his hands knew her now, the way he responded to her without question.

She clutched at him as they came together, not for balance, but because she needed him to understand that this mattered. That she wasn't choosing him blindly - she was choosing him *fully*.

Afterwards, they lay tangled in sheets, the house quiet again but changed. Tom's arm was draped over her stomach, his thumb tracing slow, absent-minded circles as if he were memorising something he feared losing.

Alice stared at the ceiling, listening to their breaths even out.

"This doesn't fix anything," she said softly.

"No," Tom replied. "But it reminds me what's worth breaking for."

She turned onto her side, facing him. "Don't say that."

"It's true."

She pressed her forehead to his chest. "I won't be protected by you destroying yourself."

His hand stilled. "I know."

But she could feel it - the thought already forming, the calculation he hadn't voiced yet.

Outside, the wind pushed through the trees, dry and insistent. Somewhere down the road, someone was burning off - controlled, permitted, safe.

Alice closed her eyes, holding onto Tom while she could, knowing that intimacy wasn't a shield.

It was a declaration.

And whatever came next, it would remember this moment - the way the land remembered everything else.

CHAPTER NINE

Alice woke to the weight of Tom's arm across her middle and the dull awareness that whatever they'd claimed last night didn't belong to them alone.

Morning light crept in through the gap in the curtains, pale and unconvincing. The house felt altered - not unsafe, not unfamiliar - just less forgiving. As if it had registered what they'd done and adjusted accordingly.

Tom stirred behind her, breath warm at her neck.

For a moment, she let herself stay exactly where she was. Anchored. Chosen. The echo of his hands still lived in her skin, a quiet reminder that last night hadn't been desperation - it had been intent.

She shifted carefully, turning onto her side to face him.

He was watching her already.

"How long have you been awake?" she asked.

"Long enough to know I didn't imagine it," he said.

She smiled faintly. "Good."

He reached out, thumb brushing her collarbone, slow and familiar. Not asking for more. Just touching because he could.

"This morning feels different," he said.

"Yes."

"Like the world noticed."

She exhaled. "That seems to be a theme."

They lay there a moment longer, bodies still close, but the urgency of the night before had softened into something heavier. This wasn't hunger now. It was reckoning.

Tom rolled onto his back and stared at the ceiling. "They've confirmed the interview time."

"When?"

"Tomorrow."

Alice pushed herself upright, pulling the sheet with her. "That's quick."

"They don't want it lingering," he said. "Neither do I."

She nodded, already feeling the slow build of resolve settle in her chest. "What will you tell them?"

"The truth," he replied. "As much of it as they ask for."

"And what they don't?"

Tom turned his head toward her. "Then I'll answer anyway."

That surprised her. She studied his face, the lines she knew so well now, the steadiness that had drawn her in long before she'd let herself admit it.

"That's new," she said.

"It is."

Silence followed - not strained, but weighted.

Alice swung her legs over the side of the bed and stood, stretching. The cool air kissed her skin, grounding her again in the ordinary. She pulled on a shirt, the ritual of dressing anchoring her back into the day.

In the kitchen, the kettle whistled too loudly. She poured the water with care.

Tom leaned against the doorway, watching her.

"You're not coming tomorrow," he said.

She turned slowly. "That wasn't a request."

"No," he agreed. "It's a boundary."

Alice crossed her arms. "I won't be kept ignorant to make this easier for you."

"I know," he said. "But this part is mine."

The words were gentle. Final.

She held his gaze, then nodded once. "For tomorrow."

His shoulders eased. "Thank you."

They ate breakfast without ceremony, talking about small things - feed, weather, the neighbour's fence - the way people did when they knew the big things would demand enough of them later.

After Tom left, Alice walked the property alone.

She followed the creek line, the one that had become the quiet spine of all this, and stopped where the concrete edge dipped beneath the water. She crouched and pressed her palm flat against the surface, feeling the cold seep in.

This was what had been hidden.

Not evil. Not cruelty.

Just people choosing themselves and believing that time would smooth it out.

Time never did.

By mid-afternoon, smoke drifted faintly on the horizon again - another burn-off, controlled and distant. Alice watched it for a long moment before turning back toward the house.

That night, Tom came to her without words.

They didn't rush. They didn't pretend this was comfort. This time, it was memory in the making.

Afterwards, as darkness settled fully around the house, Alice lay awake with Tom's hand resting over her ribs, his thumb moving in slow, absent arcs.

"You don't regret it," he said quietly.

"No."

"Even knowing where this might go?"

She turned her head enough to see his face in the low light. "Especially knowing."

He swallowed.

Outside, the land rested - dry, patient, waiting.

Alice drifted close to sleep, Tom's hand warm against her ribs, his breathing steady behind her. Just as her thoughts loosened, a faint smell reached her - smoke, distant but unmistakable.

She opened her eyes.

Down the valley, smoke lingered low in the air - not fresh, not urgent, just the trace of something already done.

Still, her chest tightened.

She lay there, listening, the echo of it sitting just beneath her skin. Smoke always meant preparation. Clearing. Making room for what came next.

Tom shifted behind her, murmuring something she didn't catch, and she forced herself to relax, to trust the ordinary.

But long after the smell faded, Alice remained awake, staring into the dark.

The land wasn't threatening her.

It was reminding her.

CHAPTER TEN

Alice knew the day would be different because she hesitated before turning the pump on.

The switch sat exactly where it always had, scuffed from years of use, reliable in the way only things that had never failed you could be. She rested her hand there longer than necessary, listening to the early morning quiet, the paddocks still holding their breath.

She didn't turn it.

Not yet.

Instead, she walked the trough line first, boots damp with dew, notebook tucked under her arm. Everything looked fine - water levels steady, stock calm, nothing urgent enough to force a decision.

That was the danger of it.

The notice had arrived two days earlier. On letterhead. Measured language. No threats. No deadlines written in red.

During the review period, landholders are advised to avoid significant changes to existing water use.

Advised. Not ordered.

Which meant interpretation.

Alice stopped at the lower trough and crouched, trailing her fingers through the surface. Clear. Cool. Enough - for now.

She stood and looked toward the creek, thinner than she liked for this time of year, the banks already showing where water used to sit longer. Nothing catastrophic. Just... less margin.

By the time Tom found her, she was leaning against the fence, notebook open but untouched.

"You haven't run it yet," he said.

"No."

He studied her face. "You're thinking."

"I'm choosing," Alice replied.

He followed her gaze to the creek. "They didn't tell you to stop."

"No, they told me to be careful."

"And?"

"And if I pretend nothing's changed," she said, "then I'm lying."

Tom exhaled slowly. "This is how it starts."

"Yes."

Not with force. With restraint.

She turned the pump on - but lower. Slower. Watching the gauge like it mattered now. Because it did.

By midday, the difference was subtle but unmistakable. Troughs filled more slowly. The rhythm she'd trusted for years shifted just enough to keep her alert.

This wasn't deprivation.

It was vigilance.

Tom leaned in the shed doorway while she recalculated paddock rotation, his presence solid and grounding and - suddenly - complicated.

"They'll watch patterns," he said.

"I know."

"And if usage drops?"

"They'll call it cooperation," Alice replied.

"And if it doesn't?"

She closed the notebook. "They'll call it defiance."

He nodded. "And which are you?"

Alice didn't answer straight away.

She looked out across Taravale - land she loved, land that had already taken more than it admitted.

"I'm honest," she said finally. "That's all I can be."

Tom's jaw tightened. "Honesty isn't neutral."

"No," she agreed. "It's expensive."

That night, when Alice lay awake listening to the pump, she understood something important.

No one had taken anything from her yet. She was the one holding back.

And the land, sensing the change, was already beginning to respond.

CHAPTER ELEVEN

The first person to say something was Mrs Calder.

Alice ran into her at the produce store in town - the kind of place where nothing ever felt accidental, even when it was. Mrs Calder had known Taravale longer than Alice had been alive. She knew its fences, its failures, its quiet years.

She reached for potatoes at the same time Alice did and paused, fingers hovering.

"Heard you're being careful with the pumps," she said mildly.

Alice straightened. "I am."

Mrs Calder nodded as if that confirmed something. "Smart. Word gets around when people aren't."

There it was.

Not accusation. Not sympathy. Just recognition.

By the time Alice reached the counter, she could feel the weight of eyes on her back. Conversations didn't stop - they softened. Shifted pitch. People watched her the way you watched weather roll in from the hills.

Curious. Measuring.

On the drive home, she passed Jack Rowley leaning against the fence line of his place, arms folded, watching her go by. He lifted two fingers in greeting - friendly enough - but didn't smile.

Jack had lost half his stock two summers ago when the creek dried earlier than anyone expected.

That wasn't coincidence. That was memory.

At Taravale, Tom was waiting by the shed.

"They're talking," he said.

Alice didn't bother asking how he knew. "How bad?"

"Not bad," Tom replied. "Yet. But it's changed."

She leaned against the ute, dust warm under her palms. "Say it."

"They're not asking what's happening," he said. "They're asking what you'll do."

That landed harder.

Alice exhaled. "And what do they think I should do?"

Tom hesitated. "They think you'll protect your own."

Alice laughed once, short and sharp. "They don't know me very well."

"No," Tom said. "They know Taravale."

That night, a ute pulled into the drive just after dark.

Alice recognised it immediately.

Maggie Rowley - Jack's sister. Hair scraped back, boots still on, no preamble in her movements. She didn't wait to be invited inside.

"Mind if I speak plainly?" Maggie asked.

Alice stepped aside. "I'd be disappointed if you didn't."

They stood on the verandah, the night thick and still around them.

"There's talk," Maggie said. "About water. About history. About who knew what."

Alice nodded. "There always is."

Maggie studied her carefully. "You're not denying it."

"I'm not pretending," Alice replied.

"That'll cost you," Maggie said.

"I know."

Maggie's mouth tightened. "Good. Because pretending cost my family everything."

The words hung there, raw and unsoftened.

Alice held her gaze. "I found something," she said quietly. "About a man who tried to speak up. Years ago."

Maggie's breath caught. Just slightly.

"Did you," she asked carefully.

"Yes."

Silence stretched between them, heavy with things neither woman had said aloud before.

"Then you should know," Maggie said finally, "that some people will hate you for dragging this back into the light."

Alice nodded. "And some won't."

Maggie's expression shifted then - not to relief, but to something like respect.

"Just don't go quiet," she said. "That's how it stays buried."

She left without another word.

Later, inside the house, Tom leaned against the bench watching Alice pace.

"They came to you," he said.

"Yes."

"That means they trust you," he added. Then, after a beat, "Or they're testing you."

"Both," Alice replied.

He studied her. "You're about to stand in the middle of this."

"I already am."

Tom nodded slowly. "Then I need to tell you something."

Here it comes, Alice thought.

"I said enough," he said quietly, "that no one's going to pretend this is small anymore."

Alice met his gaze. "Good."

Tom swallowed. "It means when people choose sides... you won't be able to choose me quietly."

The truth of that settled between them, heavy and unmistakable.

Outside, the land lay dark and patient, listening not to paperwork, but to voices - old ones, newly loud ones, rising at last.

Alice stood still, heart steady, and understood that the hardest part wasn't the pressure.

It was the visibility.

And once people started talking, there was no such thing as going back to silence.

CHAPTER TWELVE

Alice didn't sleep.

She lay awake listening to the house breathe, the sounds familiar enough to be comforting and newly altered enough to keep her alert. Somewhere after midnight, a ute passed on the road and didn't slow.

Someone else awake. Someone else thinking.

By morning, the story had already moved without her.

She heard it in the tone of the woman at the bakery - careful, friendly, newly curious. She saw it in the way a man she barely knew nodded to her outside the post office, as if acknowledging a shared understanding neither of them named.

Alice drove home with her jaw set and her hands steady on the wheel.

Visibility, she thought. That's the price.

Tom was waiting when she got back, sitting on the back steps with his elbows on his knees, hat pushed back on his head. He looked up when she parked, his expression unreadable.

"They know," he said.

"Yes."

"How bad?"

"Bad enough that pretending otherwise would be insulting."

He nodded once. "Maggie rang my sister."

That made Alice stop short. "Already?"

"Already," Tom said. "That's how this works. Stories don't travel straight. They branch."

She sat beside him, close enough that their shoulders touched. The contact was grounding and dangerous all at once.

"I won't take the quiet way out," she said.

"I didn't think you would."

"And I won't ask you to stand where people can use you against what I'm trying to do."

Tom turned his head, studying her profile. "You're not asking me to leave."

"No," Alice said. "I'm telling you what it will cost me if you stay."

The honesty of it landed harder than any ultimatum could have.

They sat there a long moment, the air between them thick with everything unsaid.

"Come inside," Tom said finally.

It wasn't a plea. It wasn't avoidance.

It was consent.

Inside, the house felt different - less like shelter, more like a witness. Alice felt it as soon as the door closed behind them, the weight of knowing that whatever happened next would be remembered by more than just the walls.

They didn't rush.

They undressed each other slowly, deliberately, as if taking inventory. Alice traced the familiar lines of Tom's shoulders, the scars she knew the stories behind, the places her hands had learned without effort.

This wasn't defiance.

This was clarity.

When they came together, it was with a tenderness that surprised her - not urgency, not fear, but recognition. Tom held her like someone who understood that holding was not the same as keeping. Alice let herself sink into it anyway, knowing exactly what she was choosing.

Afterwards, they lay tangled in the quiet, the world held at bay for just a little longer.

"This isn't a mistake," Alice said softly.

"No," Tom agreed.

She turned her head to look at him. "And tomorrow?"

"Tomorrow," he said, "you'll keep standing where you're standing."

"And you?"

Tom was quiet for a long time.

"I won't make you smaller," he said finally. "Not for me. Not for anyone."

Something in her chest tightened. "That sounds like leaving."

"It sounds like love," he replied gently.

They didn't say anything else.

Later, when Alice lay awake again, Tom's breathing steady beside her, she understood the difference between wanting and choosing.

Wanting was easy. Choosing was visible.

Outside, the land lay dark and patient, holding stories it had carried for years without comment. Somewhere down the valley, a dog barked, then fell silent. A light flicked on and off again.

People were watching now.

Alice didn't flinch.

She had chosen with her eyes open - chosen truth, chosen integrity, chosen the kind of love that didn't ask her to look away.

And whatever the land demanded next, she would meet it standing.

CHAPTER THIRTEEN

They didn't argue.

That was the part Alice would think about later - how quiet it was, how carefully they moved around each other, as if raising their voices might turn the decision into something less survivable.

Tom arrived just after dusk, the light already draining out of the paddocks. His ute pulled up near the shed, tyres crunching on gravel that hadn't quite cooled from the day. Alice watched from the kitchen window, her reflection faint against the darkening glass.

He didn't come straight inside.

She saw him pause, one hand resting on the doorframe of the ute, shoulders lifting slightly as he took a breath. As if he needed to steady himself before crossing the short distance to the house.

That, more than anything, told her this wasn't going to be a conversation they could undo.

When he came in, he didn't kiss her hello. Not out of coldness - out of care. Touch would have complicated things, and they both knew it.

"I won't stay long," he said.

Alice nodded. "I figured."

They stood in the kitchen, the familiar space suddenly formal. The kettle sat cold on the bench. Two mugs upside down in the rack, unused.

Tom glanced at them, then away.

"You found more," he said.

It wasn't a question.

"Yes."

He exhaled slowly. "How bad?"

Alice hesitated - not because she didn't know, but because naming it would make it real in a way she wasn't sure either of them was ready for.

"Bad enough," she said finally. "And old enough that pretending it's new would be dishonest."

Tom nodded once, absorbing it. "And people know you've found it."

"Some do."

"That'll become more."

"Yes."

Silence settled between them, thick but not hostile. Outside, a night bird called once and fell quiet again.

Tom leaned back against the bench, folding his arms loosely. "They'll come to you," he said. "Not loudly. Not officially. At first."

Alice watched his face as he spoke, the way he chose his words carefully, the way his jaw tightened at the edges.

"They already have," she said.

He closed his eyes briefly. "That didn't take long."

"No."

He opened them again and looked at her properly then - not searching, not assessing. Just seeing.

"This puts you in a position," he said. "And by extension..."

"By extension, you," Alice finished.

Tom shook his head. "Not just me. What I represent."

Alice swallowed. "You're not a symbol."

"In Taravale?" he said gently. "Everyone's a symbol once the story starts moving."

She didn't disagree. She couldn't.

He pushed off the bench and paced once across the room, then back again. A small movement, contained, like he was working something through in his body before saying it aloud.

"If I stay close," he said, "they'll frame this as personal. Emotional. A woman protecting her man. A man pushing her."

Alice felt something tighten in her chest. "You wouldn't."

"I know," Tom said. "But it won't matter."

She leaned back against the table, the wood cool through her shirt. "So what are you saying?"

Tom stopped pacing. He looked at her, really looked - the steadiness of him sharpened now by something harder underneath.

"I'm saying I need to step out of the frame."

Alice stared at him.

"For a while," he added quickly. "Not forever."

The words landed anyway.

She waited for the instinctive protest - the flare of anger, the urge to argue him out of it - but it didn't come. What came instead was understanding, unwelcome and immediate.

"If you're visible," she said slowly, "they can make this about us."

"Yes."

"And if you're not-"

"They lose leverage," Tom finished. "And you keep control of the narrative."

Alice let out a short breath. "So you're leaving."

Tom didn't like the word. It showed on his face. "I'm creating distance."

"You always do that when you think something's dangerous."

"I do it when I think something's worth protecting."

She closed her eyes briefly, the sting sharp but clean. "You don't get to decide what I need protecting from."

"No," he agreed. "But I do get to decide what I'm willing to risk being used against you."

She opened her eyes again. "And what about what I'm willing to risk?"

Tom held her gaze. "That's why this has to be my choice."

The quiet stretched.

Alice looked around the kitchen - the marks on the bench from years of use, the faint outline where something once hung on the wall and no longer did. This house had taught her that love didn't always announce itself loudly. Sometimes it arrived in the form of restraint.

"How far is distance?" she asked.

"Enough," Tom said. "I won't be here. I won't be seen. I won't be the reason anyone doubts your decisions."

"And if I need you?"

His expression softened. "You call. And I'll come if it's about you - not the story."

Alice nodded, though it hurt. "You'll help without being seen."

"Yes."

She looked at him then, really looked - the man who had stood beside her through the slow, difficult process of returning, who had learned the land with her instead of ahead of her.

"You're choosing to leave me alone in this," she said quietly.

Tom stepped closer, stopping just short of touching her. "I'm choosing not to make you choose between truth and us."

Her throat tightened. "You don't think I would?"

"I think you'd try to carry both," he said. "And I won't let that be the cost."

For a moment - just a moment - Alice thought he might falter. Thought he might reach for her and undo everything he'd just said.

He didn't.

Instead, he reached into his pocket and pulled out a folded piece of paper, placing it on the table between them.

"Contacts," he said. "People you might need. Contractors. Surveyors. A couple of names you won't want to use unless you have to."

She stared at the paper. "You've been preparing for this."

"Yes."

"How long?"

"Since the first time you said you wouldn't let it go."

A strange mix of grief and pride washed through her. "You knew me better than I did."

He smiled faintly. "I hoped."

Alice picked up the paper and folded it carefully, tucking it into her pocket. "When?"

"Tonight," Tom said. "I'll take a few things now. The rest can wait."

She nodded, the motion stiff.

They moved around each other then, collecting small, practical items. A bag. A jacket. His boots from beside the door.

The domesticity of it made something inside her ache more than the words had.

When he stood at the door, hand on the frame, Alice finally stepped closer.

"This isn't over," she said.

Tom met her eyes. "No."

"But it's not together either."

"For now," he said.

She hesitated, then leaned in and rested her forehead briefly against his chest - just long enough to feel his breath steady and familiar.

"Be careful," she said.

Tom's hand hovered near her shoulder, then settled there gently. "You too."

He left without looking back.

Alice stood in the doorway long after the sound of his ute faded, the night closing in around the house.

Distance, she thought, was not the same as absence.

But it demanded the same strength.

And tonight, she would have to find that strength without him beside her.

CHAPTER FOURTEEN

Alice didn't go looking for it.

That mattered to her later - the knowledge that she hadn't set out to excavate the past, hadn't come armed with suspicion or righteous certainty. She had come to fix a hinge. A small, practical job. The kind of thing you did when you needed your hands occupied and your thoughts quiet.

The shed was cool despite the heat outside, the thick air holding the smells it always had: oil, dust, old timber. Light filtered in through the high window, catching on motes that drifted lazily, undisturbed.

She worked methodically, grounding herself in the familiar rhythm - loosen, adjust, tighten. Metal scraped softly. The hinge resisted, then shifted, as if finally deciding to cooperate.

That was when she noticed the box.

It sat tucked behind a stack of old seed bags, half-hidden, its edges softened by time. Alice frowned slightly. She didn't remember putting it there. She didn't remember *seeing* it at all.

She told herself that meant nothing.

Taravale was full of things she hadn't placed and hadn't noticed - the accumulation of years, of other hands, of decisions made long before she arrived with adult eyes.

Still, when she reached for the box, she felt a small, involuntary hesitation.

It was heavier than it should have been.

Not impossibly so - just enough to register. Enough to unsettle.

Alice dragged it into the light and crouched beside it, dust puffing up around her knees. The lid was unmarked. No label. No handwriting. Just plain cardboard, warped slightly at the corners.

She rested her hand on the top and paused.

There was no sense of drama. No instinctive fear. Just the faint awareness that once opened, it couldn't be unopened.

She lifted the lid.

Photographs lay inside, loose and curled, their edges soft with age. Alice picked up the first one carefully, as if the paper might bruise.

A man stood beside the creek.

He was younger than she'd expected - mid-thirties, perhaps - sleeves rolled to the elbow, boots sunk into damp soil. He wasn't looking at the camera. His head was turned slightly, mouth open as if caught mid-sentence.

Alive, Alice thought.

The realisation landed hard enough to knock the breath from her lungs.

She set the photo aside and reached for another.

The same man again, this time with two children. A boy and a girl, both barefoot, both smiling with the easy confidence of kids who believed the world was solid beneath them. The land behind them was unmistakable - the bend of the creek Alice knew as well as her own hands.

Her fingers tightened around the edge of the photo.

She knew that place.

She knew that waterline.

Beneath the photographs lay letters.

They were folded thin from handling, the paper creased and re-creased as if the act of opening them had once been compulsive. Alice hesitated, then unfolded the first one slowly.

The water's not running like it used to. They say it's seasonal, but I've lived here my whole life. This isn't that.

Her throat tightened.

She read the next.

I went to speak to them again. They told me I was mistaken. That the maps don't show what I'm seeing. I know what this land looks like when it's lying.

Alice lowered herself onto an overturned crate, the concrete seeping cold through her jeans. Her hands were shaking now, noticeably so. She pressed her palms together once, hard, grounding herself.

The third letter was shorter.

If something happens to me, it won't be an accident. I won't stop asking.

A sharp wave of nausea rolled through her, sudden and disorienting. Alice leaned forward, elbows braced on her knees, breathing carefully until the sensation eased.

This wasn't paranoia.

This was pattern.

At the bottom of the box lay something heavier.

A notebook. Small. Soft-cover. The edges darkened with use. Alice flipped it open at random.

Hand-drawn lines filled the pages - creek paths, measurements, annotations scrawled in the margins. Dates repeated. Levels marked and re-marked.

Evidence, she realised.

Careful. Patient. Ignored.

The final photograph lay beneath the notebook.

The man again - this time in a hospital bed, eyes closed, a bandage wrapped around his head. The photo was poorly taken, too close, as if the person behind the camera hadn't been allowed to linger.

Alice turned it over.

They said he slipped.

That was all.

Her breath left her in a rush she hadn't authorised.

She sat there for a long time, the open box at her feet, the shed holding its breath around her. No birds. No wind. Just the thick, stunned quiet of something that had waited years to be seen.

This wasn't negligence.

This wasn't oversight.

This was pressure applied until resistance became dangerous.

This was silence enforced by exhaustion.

Alice pressed the heel of her hand into her sternum, steadying herself against the urge to rage, to cry, to undo something that could not be undone.

When she finally stood, her legs trembled - not with weakness, but with resolve settling into place.

She carried the box into the house and laid everything out on the dining table. She didn't rush. She studied each face, each line of handwriting, until the man became real to her - not a symbol, not a story, but a person who had stood on land and told the truth when it would have been easier not to.

Outside, the wind picked up, rattling the windows faintly.

Borrowed water, she thought. Borrowed silence.

Alice closed the notebook and reached for her phone.

She didn't call Tom. She didn't call anyone official.

She called Maggie Rowley.

"I found something," Alice said when Maggie answered. Her voice was steady, though it felt like it was made of glass. "And I think it belongs to you."

There was a pause on the line. A breath caught, then released.

"I've been waiting a long time for that call," Maggie said quietly.

Alice closed her eyes.

When she hung up, she stood alone in the kitchen, the weight of the discovery settling into her bones.

This was what the land had kept.

Not water. Not power.

A story that refused to stay buried.

And Alice understood, with a clarity that left no room for retreat, that whatever the land left her in the end, it would include this truth - carried forward, named aloud, and never put back in the dark.

CHAPTER FIFTEEN

Alice left the papers on the table like they were capable of moving on their own.

Photographs in one loose pile, letters in another, the notebook open at the page she'd landed on - the creek bend sketched and re-sketched, measurements written and rewritten as if the act of recording could force the world to behave.

She stood in the kitchen and stared at it all, hands resting on the back of a chair she didn't sit in.

Outside, the late light caught the windows. Inside, the house held its breath.

She should have packed it away. She knew that. She should have put it back in the box, closed the lid, and walked out to check troughs or gates or anything with a simple purpose. Something she could fix with her hands.

Instead of defaulting to motion, Alice stayed still.
The kitchen held the quiet badly - every sound too sharp, every surface too aware of her.

She reached for the kettle out of habit, switched it on, then turned it off again before it boiled. The small click echoed more than it should have.

Her phone lay on the bench, face down. She didn't touch it.

Maggie's voice surfaced - remembered, not replayed.

I've been waiting a long time for that call.

The weight of it settled differently now, stripped of the softness Maggie had used at the time.

Alice had swallowed and managed, *I'll bring it over.*

No, Maggie had replied softly, and the softness had been the hardest part. *Don't bring it anywhere yet. Not until we talk.*

Alice realised she'd been holding her breath.

Now, in the kitchen, she let it out slowly, and looked back at the table.

The man in the photograph didn't look like a symbol. He looked like someone who'd laughed loudly, who'd gotten sunburnt on the back of his neck, who'd thought he'd done the sensible thing by writing things down.

The letters weren't dramatic. That was what chilled her. They were practical, measured, the handwriting steady - the voice of someone who still believed systems responded to facts.

Alice picked up the first page again and read it from the beginning, even though she already knew it by heart now.

The water's not running like it used to.

She read the next one, slower.

They told me I was mistaken. That the maps don't show what I'm seeing.

Her stomach twisted.

Maps, she thought. That old confidence. That belief that if something wasn't recorded officially, it wasn't real.

She turned the notebook page and found a margin note she hadn't noticed earlier.

If I stop, it becomes true.

Alice stared at the line for a long time.

If I stop, it becomes true.

It wasn't about water anymore. It wasn't even about being right. It was about being erased. About letting someone else decide what counted as reality.

Alice put the notebook down and stood, chair scraping faintly against the floor.

The house felt smaller suddenly.

Not claustrophobic - just... aware. Like it knew what had been laid out on its table. Like it was judging her for the way her hands were trembling, for the way she kept glancing at the hallway, as if something might step out of it.

She walked down to the closed room - the one that had been locked up when she arrived back at Taravale, the one that had been part of the house's long habit of hiding. For the last year, it had stayed open, ordinary, harmless.

She stood at the doorway and looked in.

Nothing moved. Nothing waited.

Just a room.

And still, she felt the faint prickle of that same old message: *Some things are better left alone.*

Alice stepped inside anyway.

She stood in the middle of it and listened to the silence settle around her. Not ominous. Not mystical. Just quiet. The kind of quiet that made thoughts louder.

She turned back out and returned to the kitchen like someone choosing daylight.

The urge to call Tom hit her unexpectedly - not a plan, not a decision. Just instinct. The old reflex of reaching for the one person who made the world feel less sharp around the edges.

She picked up her phone.

Thumb hovered.

She could picture him too clearly: his hands, the way he leaned in a doorway as if he belonged there, the steadiness of him. She could picture the relief she would feel hearing his voice. That relief would be real.

And temporary.

Because if she told him, she couldn't untell him. If she pulled him into this, it wouldn't be a choice he got to make later. It would be a consequence delivered through love.

Alice set the phone down again as if it were hot.

"No," she said aloud, and the word steadied her more than it should have.

She wasn't protecting him from the truth.

She was protecting the truth from becoming about him.

She moved through the house restlessly, opening cupboards she didn't need, wiping a bench that was already clean, feeding the dog even though the bowl was still half full. She checked the back door lock twice, then caught herself and stopped.

Fear, she reminded herself, was a habit. Vigilance was a decision.

When she finally sat down at the table again, she forced herself to read every page properly.

Names appeared more than once.

Not in dramatic ways. In familiar ways. The kind of names you'd heard at barbecues. The kind of names you'd seen on plaques at the showground. The kind of names that felt like community until they didn't.

Alice's throat tightened as she realised what that meant.

This wasn't a story about one bad man.

It was a story about a whole place deciding, quietly, what it would tolerate.

She sat very still, the mug cooling beside her, and let that truth settle into her bones.

Outside, evening deepened. The air shifted, a faint warm wind slipping through the flyscreen. Leaves brushed against the side of the house like soft fingers.

Alice stood and took the box back into her arms.

She carried it out to the verandah and sat on the top step with it pressed against her knees, like a child guarding something that didn't belong to them.

The sky was turning that pale, bruised colour it got after hot days - washed out, hesitant, as if it couldn't decide whether to be beautiful or warning.

Down the valley, a dog barked once and fell silent.

A ute passed on the road, headlights sweeping briefly across the paddock.

Someone out there, she thought, moving through the same dark. Someone with their own version of this story. Someone who already knew.

Her phone vibrated again.

A message from Maggie.

Don't leave it in the house tonight. Not because of thieves. Because of people. Come in the morning. Early.

Alice read it twice.

People.

The word sat heavy in her mouth.

She looked back toward the house behind her. The windows were dark. The kitchen table waited inside, the papers laid out like a confession.

Alice stood, box in her arms, and walked to the ute.

She didn't put it in the tray.

She put it behind the driver's seat, where it would be hard to see without climbing in. She covered it with an old jacket and stood there for a moment, hand resting on the doorframe, breathing slowly.

This was real now.

Not theory. Not suspicion. Not grief.

Real.

She locked the ute, then walked back to the verandah and sat down again, hands clasped, looking out over Taravale as the first stars appeared.

The land lay quiet, indifferent to what it had just done - to what it had handed her.

Alice thought about the man in the photos, writing his notes, marking lines, measuring water. She thought about him going to speak, being told he was wrong, going back again anyway.

If I stop, it becomes true.

Alice swallowed hard.

She didn't know yet what the offer would look like - only that it would come. She could already feel the shape of it in the air: the soft voice, the reasonable tone, the gentle promise that things could return to normal if she would just cooperate.

She let herself imagine it for one brief moment - how it would feel to say yes. To fold the papers away. To let the land keep what it kept. To keep Tom at a distance from the ugliness of it.

A version of peace.

Then she pictured the man's handwriting again. The photograph of him in hospital. The sentence on the back: *They said he slipped.*

And she felt something harden quietly inside her.

Not anger.

Clarity.

Alice stood, went inside, and turned off every light except the one over the kitchen table. She sat down and arranged the pages neatly, as if order could lend courage.

Then she wrote a single line on a fresh piece of paper - for herself, not for anyone else.

I will not make myself small to keep other people comfortable.

She stared at it until her eyes burned.

Outside, the creek kept running, unseen in the dark.

Inside, Alice finally drank her tea - cold, grounding - and understood that the land hadn't asked her a question.

It had handed her an answer.

And tomorrow, someone would come offering her a way to put it back.

CHAPTER SIXTEEN

The next morning arrived too clean.

Sunlight poured across the kitchen as if nothing had changed, as if the land hadn't handed Alice a story heavy enough to change the shape of her life. The house smelled faintly of dust warmed by early heat, the kind of smell that usually meant routine, not reckoning.

Alice made tea properly this time - not because she wanted it, but because hot water and a mug in her hands gave her something to do while her thoughts kept circling.

She set the cup on the bench and stood at the window, watching the driveway.

It was a ridiculous habit, she told herself. The country taught you to notice movement - a car, a horse, a neighbour at a gate - but this felt different. This was waiting.

She heard tyres on gravel just after nine.

A white SUV rolled up the drive at a careful speed. Not a local ute. Not someone arriving with casual confidence. The vehicle stopped well short of the verandah, as if the driver wanted room to retreat without turning around.

Alice watched the door open.

A man stepped out, mid-fifties, neat collared shirt, boots that had never seen mud. He held his hat in his hands as he approached the house, posture respectful, expression arranged into something that would pass for warmth.

He stopped at the bottom of the verandah steps.

"Alice," he called, not too loud. Like he didn't want the land hearing.

She stepped outside, keeping the screen door closed behind her. Not locked - just... a boundary.

"Can I help you?" she asked.

The man's smile widened slightly. "Graham O'Neill."

The name was familiar in the way some names were - never close, but always present. At events, on committees, on local fundraising posters. A man who knew how to be useful in public.

"I know who you are," Alice said.

Graham nodded, pleased, then quickly smoothed it into humility. "Right. Well. I won't take much of your time."

Alice didn't invite him up the steps.

He seemed to register it, and adjusted his stance, still holding his hat like an offering.

"I heard there was a bit of trouble," he said.

Alice stared at him. "You heard."

He gave a small, careful laugh, the kind that implied he understood how gossip worked without admitting he participated. "Town's a small place. News travels."

Alice waited.

Graham cleared his throat. "I've been asked to check in. Make sure you're... supported."

By who, Alice thought, but she didn't say it. She let the silence do its work.

Graham shifted, then leaned slightly into sincerity. "You've had a lot on. The property, the drought. And now, whatever it is you've found."

Alice's stomach tightened.

Whatever it is you've found.

The polite way of saying: *We know.*

Her voice stayed even. "If you don't know what it is, you can't be very helpful."

Graham's smile flickered. "Fair point."

He glanced down briefly, then back up, as if taking his cues from her face. "Look, Alice… people are concerned this could get… complicated."

Alice's eyes narrowed slightly. "Complicated for who?"

Graham exhaled, patient. "For everyone. For you, too."

Alice held his gaze. "If you're here to tell me it's better not to talk about it, you're wasting your morning."

He lifted one hand, palm out. "No, no. Not that." Then, carefully: "I'm here to suggest there might be a way to handle it… quietly."

There it was.

Quietly.

The word sat between them like a familiar tool.

Graham continued, "These things have a way of turning into... narratives. Headlines. People taking sides. Families dragged through mud. You don't want that."

Alice didn't answer.

"You're young," he added, as if it were kindness. "You've got a future here. You've got the property. You've got your reputation. The community. It would be a shame to-"

"To what?" Alice asked. "To lose it?"

Graham's smile returned, relieved to be in a question-answer structure. "To damage it unnecessarily, yes."

Alice's chest tightened. "Damage. Like what happened to the man in those photos?"

Graham's eyes sharpened for the first time. Not anger - calculation. He recovered quickly, expression smoothing back into concern.

"We don't know the full circumstances," he said softly. "And that's exactly the problem. People read things into events. Mistakes get made."

Alice felt her jaw set. "You're saying he slipped."

Graham's throat bobbed. "I'm saying I wasn't there. None of us were."

"You were here," Alice said, and watched his face react before he could control it. "You were in this town. On the committees. At the meetings. You were *around*."

Graham's smile became thinner, more professional. "Alice, what I'm trying to do is protect you from becoming the centre of a war you don't need."

Alice let out a small breath. "I didn't choose to be the centre."

"No," he agreed quickly. "But you can choose how you respond."

There it was again.

Choice, framed as freedom, offered like a gift while the weight of consequence hung behind it.

Graham stepped one pace closer to the verandah steps, still not climbing them, still signalling respect. "There are options," he said. "A path where you don't have to carry this alone.

Where your concerns are heard. Where we can... resolve it."

Alice's mouth tightened. "Resolve it how?"

Graham's voice softened. "Privately. There are people willing to come to the table. To make amends."

"Amends," Alice repeated, tasting the word. "That's an interesting way to say 'keep it contained.'"

Graham's smile didn't reach his eyes. "Contained isn't always a bad thing. Some things-"

"Some things are better left alone," Alice finished quietly.

Graham blinked, surprised, as if he hadn't expected her to name the subtext so cleanly.

Alice stepped down onto the verandah boards, bringing herself closer without inviting him in. She looked at him steadily.

"Do you know why I won't do this quietly?" she asked.

Graham hesitated. "Because you're angry?"

"No," Alice said. "Because quiet is what let it happen."

Graham's face tightened. "That's not fair."

Alice shrugged slightly. "Maybe not. But it's true."

He exhaled, the first hint of frustration breaking through. "Alice, if you push this out into the open, you won't get control back. People will take it from you. The story won't belong to you anymore."

Alice felt something cold and steady settle in her chest.

"That," she said, "is exactly why I'm not handing it back to the people who kept it quiet in the first place."

Graham's gaze flicked toward the house, as if he wanted to see inside, to assess what she had, what she knew. Alice didn't move.

He looked back at her and tried a different angle - gentler, almost fatherly.

"You've been through a lot already," he said. "You don't need to be the hero."

Alice's throat tightened. "I'm not trying to be a hero."

"Then what are you trying to be?"

Alice held his gaze. "Honest."

For a moment, Graham said nothing.

Then he nodded slowly, as if accepting the inevitability of her stubbornness, and put his hat back on.

"Alright," he said. "I've said what I came to say."

Alice didn't respond.

Graham stepped back toward his SUV, gravel crunching under his boots. Before he opened the door, he turned.

"Just... think," he said. "There are people who can make this easier."

Alice kept her voice calm. "If it was easy, someone would have done it years ago."

Graham's mouth tightened. He nodded once, stiffly, and climbed into the car.

The SUV rolled back down the drive and disappeared in a quiet cloud of dust.

Alice stood on the verandah for a long moment, listening to the aftermath of the encounter settle.

Polite pressure.

That was what Taravale did first - not threats, not force. Just calm suggestions delivered by people with clean boots and community roles, framed as care.

She went back inside and closed the door.

Her tea sat untouched where she'd left it.

Alice picked up the mug, took one sip, and grimaced. It had gone bitter.

She poured it out and rinsed the cup, the water running clear over porcelain, over her fingers, over the small tremor that had returned now that the conversation was over.

Then she dried her hands slowly, deliberately, and looked at the phone on the bench.

Not to call Tom.

Not to call anyone.

Just to remind herself what came next.

Because if that was the quiet approach...

...the official offer wouldn't be gentle.

CHAPTER SEVENTEEN

The meeting didn't feel like a meeting.

That was the first thing Alice noticed.

No boardroom. No files spread across a table. Just two chairs on a verandah that wasn't hers, a pot of tea already poured, steam lifting gently into the late afternoon air.

Maggie Rowley sat opposite her, hands wrapped around her cup. She looked older than Alice remembered - not in years, but in weight. Some losses aged you sideways.

"I wasn't sure you'd come," Maggie said.

"I wasn't sure I should," Alice replied.

They shared a look that acknowledged how little certainty either of them had left.

Maggie glanced toward the paddocks, then back. "People are nervous."

"Yes," Alice said. "They should be."

Maggie didn't argue. "There's concern this will turn into something bigger than anyone can control."

Alice smiled faintly. "It already has."

That earned her a soft huff of laughter.

"I didn't bring you here to scare you," Maggie said. "I brought you because you deserve to know what's being said out loud."

"And what's that?"

"That you don't owe this land your ruin," Maggie replied carefully.

Alice tilted her head. "That's an interesting way to start."

Maggie set her cup down. "There's a path forward being discussed. Quiet. Contained. No one dragged through the mud."

Alice waited.

"You acknowledge historical complexity," Maggie continued. "You agree the past is murky. You commit to cooperation, improvement, and discretion."

"And?"

"And the story stops growing," Maggie said. "No headlines. No names spoken aloud. No families reopening old wounds."

Alice felt the shape of it before Maggie said the rest.

"And in return?"

Maggie met her gaze steadily. "Taravale survives intact. You keep the land. You keep your life."

Alice leaned back in her chair, the boards creaking beneath her weight. "And the man who died?"

Maggie looked away. "He stays where he is."

Silence stretched between them, heavy and unforgiving.

"This isn't justice," Alice said quietly.

"No," Maggie agreed. "It's mercy."

"For who?"

"For everyone still standing," Maggie replied. "Including you."

Alice watched the light shift across the paddock, the long shadows stretching as the sun dipped lower. She thought about the box on her dining table. About the letters folded thin with use. About the way the land kept what suited it and discarded the rest.

"And Tom?" Alice asked.

Maggie hesitated just long enough to answer the question Alice hadn't fully voiced.

"It would help," she said, "if his name didn't keep surfacing alongside yours."

There it was.

Not a demand. A suggestion.

Alice nodded slowly. "So silence. Survival. Separation."

Maggie winced. "I wouldn't put it that way."

"I would," Alice replied. "Because words matter."

They sat there for a long moment, the air thick with what could be avoided.

"You'd be doing the sensible thing," Maggie said gently. "Most people would."

Alice smiled then - not kindly, not bitterly. Just honestly.

"That's what worries me."

Maggie searched her face. "You don't have to be the one who carries this."

Alice leaned forward, resting her forearms on her knees. "I already am."

She stood, the decision settling into her bones with surprising calm.

"I won't keep him buried," she said. "And I won't pretend the land didn't benefit."

Maggie exhaled slowly, as if she'd known this would be the answer but had hoped anyway.

"Then it will get harder," she said.

"I know."

"And lonelier."

"I know."

Maggie nodded once. "If it helps," she said quietly, "some of us will remember who didn't look away."

Alice met her gaze. "That will have to be enough."

She left before the tea cooled completely.

On the drive home, the sky burned gold and red over the paddocks, the heat lingering even as the light faded. Alice drove with the windows down, the air heavy and dry against her skin.

This was how the land tested you, she thought.

Not with disaster.

With the offer to make it all go away.

And as Taravale came into view, Alice understood with steady certainty that she hadn't chosen difficulty.

She'd chosen truth.

And now the land would answer in its own time.

CHAPTER EIGHTEEN

The fallout didn't arrive loudly.

It slid in through the ordinary places first - the shop, the road, the pauses where people usually filled silence without thinking. It came in the way conversations adjusted when Alice entered a room, not stopping, just... changing shape. Like a creek diverting around a rock.

Alice noticed it at the gates.

A neighbour who usually lifted two fingers from the steering wheel didn't. Another slowed, then drove on without stopping, eyes forward as if he hadn't seen her at all. Someone left a box of excess pumpkins at the end of her drive with no note, no name - kindness delivered anonymously, as if being seen offering it might carry risk.

Support that had to be disguised.

By the time she reached town, she'd already rehearsed what she would and wouldn't say. Not because she was afraid of questions, but because she'd learned that answering the wrong one gave people something to carry away and reshape.

The produce store smelled like dust and oranges and old timber. The doorbell chimed as she walked in, too bright for the careful quiet that followed.

Linda was behind the counter. She smiled a little too fast.

"Morning," Linda said. "You right?"

Alice met her eyes. "I'm standing."

Linda nodded, the smile slipping into something more honest. "Good."

Two women by the fridges paused mid-sentence. Not silence - just a hitch, like a breath taken at the wrong time.

Alice moved through the aisles slowly. Flour. Salt. Tea. The dull, controllable things.

As she reached for sugar, a voice behind her said, "Heard you're making a mess of things."

Alice finished placing the bag into her basket before turning.

Kerry Haines stood there, arms folded, brittle smile firmly in place.

"Is that what you heard?" Alice asked.

Kerry shrugged. "People are saying you've stirred up old trouble. That there was peace for a reason."

"Peace for who?" Alice asked calmly.

"For everyone."

"That's funny," Alice said. "Because the man in those photos didn't get much peace at all."

The air shifted. Linda stilled. The women by the fridges suddenly became very interested in eggs.

"You don't know the full story," Kerry said.

"No I don't," Alice replied. "That's the point."

Kerry scoffed. "You'll cost people their livelihoods."

"I'm not the one who did it," Alice said. "I'm just refusing to keep pretending it didn't happen."

Kerry flushed. "Some of us don't want our kids dragged into this."

"Then don't teach them silence is safety."

Kerry opened her mouth, closed it again, then turned away.

At the counter, Linda rang Alice up too quickly.

"I'm sorry," she murmured, eyes on the register.

"For what?"

"For... people."

Alice softened. "You don't have to apologise for other people."

Linda swallowed. "You're brave. It makes the rest of us look like cowards."

"No," Alice said gently. "It makes us human."

Outside, Jack Rowley leaned against his ute across the road.

"You didn't have to come into town today," he said when she joined him.

"I don't lay low."

"No," Jack agreed. "You don't."

They stood together, watching a car roll past too slowly.

"You didn't take the offer," Jack said.

"No."

"That'll make things harder."

"Yes."

A pause.

"Old man wouldn't have kept quiet either," Jack said finally.

Something loosened in Alice's chest. "Thank you."

Jack nodded. "Working bee tomorrow. Fire prep."

"I'll be there."

He studied her. "You don't have to."

"I know."

The next morning arrived already warm.

Utes lined the fence at McAllister's place. Chainsaws, gloves, rakes piled together. People stood in loose groups, talking weather and grass and anything but why they were there.

Alice arrived and picked up a rake without ceremony.

Work came easily. Clearing scrub. Dragging branches. Widening the break.

She worked beside people she'd known forever and people who barely looked at her. Tools were passed without comment. Instructions followed without debate.

Fire didn't care who you voted for.

She ended up beside Kerry again.

"You didn't have to show up," Kerry said sharply.

"Neither did you."

They worked in silence until Kerry said, "People are worried."

"I know."

"You've put everyone on edge."

"The edge was already there."

"It won't end cleanly."

"No," Alice agreed. "It never does."

By midmorning, heat pressed down. Bottles were passed from the esky.

"Glad you came," a woman said quietly, then looked away.

Jack checked the wind, frowning. "It's shifting."

"I can feel it," Alice said.

"Some folks think you complicate things."

"Fire doesn't choose sides," Alice replied. "I'll still hold a hose."

Jack nodded. "That's what matters."

As people packed up, Alice overheard fragments.

"...should've been dealt with years ago-"

"...not her fault, but still-"

"...fire'll sort it out-"

Fire sorted nothing. It only revealed what was already dry.

When Alice reached her ute, the note was tucked under the wiper.

YOU'RE STIRRING THINGS THAT WERE SETTLED.

She folded it carefully. Information, not fear.

At home, a box waited on the verandah.

Dog biscuits. Electrolytes. Baby wipes. Care, delivered quietly.

That evening, Maggie rang.

"You've upset the balance," she said.

"Balance for who?"

"For people who thought the cost had already been paid."

"It was postponed."

"Yes," Maggie agreed. "And postponement feels like peace."

Alice stood at the fence as dusk settled, the ground too dry beneath her boots.

This was consequence without drama. Watchfulness. Withdrawal. Quiet alignment.

She squared her shoulders and turned back toward the house.

Let them watch.

She wasn't going anywhere.

CHAPTER NINETEEN

The house always sounded different after town.

Not louder - quieter, in a way that made Alice notice every small noise she normally ignored. The fridge hum. A fly tapping at the window. The slight creak of floorboards as the timber cooled.

She came in through the back door and stood for a moment with her hand on the latch, as if she could feel the day still clinging to her skin.

Town had been careful. So had she.

That was what exhausted her most - not the confrontation with Kerry, not the sidelong looks, not even the anonymous note folded in her pocket like a threat trying to pass as information.

It was the restraint.

The constant calculation of what to say, what not to say, where to stand, where to look, how to exist in a place that had decided she was now a story instead of a person.

Alice set the groceries on the bench and unpacked them slowly, deliberately. Flour into the pantry. Tea beside the kettle. Sugar into the jar. The small rituals steadied her hands.

She pulled the note out of her pocket and placed it on the table.

It looked ridiculous in the kitchen light. A square of paper pretending it held power.

YOU'RE STIRRING THINGS THAT WERE SETTLED.

Alice stared at the sentence until it lost meaning and became shapes.

Settled.

Like silt. Like mud. Like something that sank when you stopped disturbing the water.

She thought of the man's handwriting in the notebook. The way he'd measured and recorded and refused to accept that the land he knew could be overwritten by a map.

If I stop, it becomes true.

Alice folded the note once, twice, then slid it into the drawer with the spare batteries and old receipts. Not hiding it. Filing it.

Information, she reminded herself again.

She opened the fridge and realised she wasn't hungry. Her stomach had been tight all day, as if her body had decided eating was optional now that it was busy surviving.

She forced herself to pull out bread and cheese anyway, made a sandwich she barely tasted, and ate it standing at the sink.

Outside, the last of the light drained away, leaving the paddocks washed in blue-grey. The sky held that brittle clarity it got before wind.

Alice rinsed her plate, wiped the bench again though it was already clean, and finally allowed herself to stop moving.

That was when the loneliness arrived properly.

Not as sadness - not yet - but as absence with weight. The awareness of how big the house could feel when there was only one person inside it. How every room held the echo of what it used to contain.

Tom would have noticed the note immediately. He would have read it, looked at her, said something simple that made it feel manageable.

He wasn't here.

Alice walked to the verandah and stepped outside, leaning on the rail.

The land lay still. The creek was a dark line of sound more than sight. Somewhere down the valley, a dog barked once, then fell silent.

She stared out toward the boundary until her eyes ached, as if she could will the world back into a shape she recognised.

Her phone sat in her pocket.

She didn't take it out.

She didn't want the comfort. That was the truth of it. Comfort was not neutral - it came with strings, with consequences, with a pull backward into the old pattern where Tom steadied her and she let him.

This time, she needed to stand on her own feet.

Still, the urge to reach out was sharp enough to feel physical.

Alice walked back inside and turned on the light over the kitchen table.

She pulled out the papers again - the photographs, the letters, the notebook. She hadn't planned to. She told herself she was checking details.

But the truth was simpler.

Looking at them reminded her why she couldn't stop.

She spread the pages out neatly, her movements controlled, almost reverent. She read a letter again, slower this time, noticing the way the handwriting changed halfway through the page - the letters narrowing, the ink darker. A day when the man had pressed harder.

She flipped through the notebook and found a line she'd missed earlier, tucked into a margin near a date:

They want me tired.

Alice stared at it, and something cold settled into her chest.

That was the strategy, wasn't it?

Not to defeat you in one clean blow.

To exhaust you. To make you doubt yourself. To make you crave quiet so badly you'd trade truth for relief.

Alice set the notebook down and pressed her fingers against her eyes until she saw stars.

When she lowered her hands, she realised she was shaking again.

Not fear, exactly.

Adrenaline with nowhere to go.

She stood and walked to the hallway, then stopped.

The house was too still. The closed-room door stood open now, ordinary, empty. The old stone walls held the night coolly, indifferent to her discomfort.

Alice went to the laundry and pulled out a blanket, then returned to the lounge.

She didn't turn on the television. She didn't want noise. She wanted the night to be what it was - a test of whether she could sit with herself without reaching for someone else.

She lay on the couch with the blanket over her legs and stared at the ceiling.

Minutes passed.

Then an hour.

Her mind replayed the day in fragments.

Kerry's face in the shop. The way the women by the fridges had stopped mid-sentence. Linda's confession - brave, coward, human. Jack's steady nod. The working bee, people standing shoulder-to-shoulder without offering warmth.

And then the note.

Settled.

The word pulsed at the back of her mind like a bruise.

Alice closed her eyes and tried to sleep.

She couldn't.

Every time she drifted, her mind snapped back to the same point: the feeling that something else was moving beneath the surface, quiet but purposeful.

A memory surfaced - her mother once telling her that in small towns, people didn't shout. They *withdrew*. They starved you of normal until you started begging for it.

Alice turned onto her side, blanket tightening around her legs.

She wanted to cry.

Not because she regretted it.

Because she knew what it would cost.

She lay there and let the feeling move through her without fighting it, without turning it into drama. Just grief, plain and sharp, for the simplicity she had lost.

Eventually, she sat up and reached for her phone.

Not to call Tom.

Just to check the time.

1:17 a.m.

Alice stared at the numbers as if they could offer a solution.

Then the screen lit with a new message.

Unknown number.

No greeting. No name.

You don't know what you're playing with.

Alice's stomach dropped.

She read it again, slower.

Same message.

No further context.

She stared at it until the screen dimmed.

This wasn't town gossip anymore. This wasn't social discomfort. This was someone stepping closer.

Her hand tightened around the phone.

For one breath - one sharp, instinctive breath - she almost called Tom.

She could picture it: his voice, immediate, awake, steady. The way he'd say her name like a promise.

Alice's thumb hovered over his contact.

Then she lowered the phone.

Not yet, she told herself.

Not because he didn't deserve to know.

Because if she brought him in now, this would become exactly what Tom had warned her about: a story with a man at its centre, a woman framed as emotional, unstable, led.

No.

Alice stood and walked into the kitchen, turning on the light. The harsh brightness steadied her. She wrote the message down on a notepad beside the kettle, copying it exactly.

Then she wrote the time.

Then she wrote one more line beneath it:

Escalation.

She stared at the word.

And then - because she would not be kept awake by unnamed people and vague threats - she did something simple, practical, and stubborn.

She made tea.

The kettle boiled. The mug warmed her palms. This time, she drank.

The bitterness grounded her, the heat settling her body back into itself.

Alice turned off the lights room by room, leaving only the kitchen lamp on. Not because she was afraid of the dark, but because she wanted one place in the house that felt held.

She lay down in her bed fully clothed, phone on the bedside table, the papers on the kitchen table behind her like a presence she couldn't ignore.

Outside, the wind rose slightly, brushing the gumtrees, moving over the paddocks with a dry, impatient sound.

Alice closed her eyes and forced herself to breathe slowly, deliberately.

Whatever was moving beneath Taravale's surface, it had started to show itself now.

And Alice understood, with a calm that surprised her, that the real fight wasn't going to be loud.

It was going to be steady.

It was going to be long.

And she was not going to be worn down into quiet.

CHAPTER TWENTY

The heat arrived early.

Not the brutal kind - not yet - but the wrong kind. The kind that crept in overnight and lingered through the morning, settling into the soil instead of lifting with the breeze.

Alice felt it the moment she stepped outside.

The air was already tight, unmoving, carrying the faint smell of dust and something sharper underneath. Dry grass crunched under her boots where it should have bent. Leaves curled slightly at the edges, conserving what little moisture they had left.

She checked the weather without expecting comfort.

Hotter. Wind later. No rain in sight.

She closed the app and went back to work.

The days had taken on a new rhythm since Tom left. Longer. Quieter. Less forgiving. There was no one to hand a thought to halfway through forming it, no second pair of eyes to catch what she missed when fatigue crept in.

Alice noticed small things now - the way the fence line near the south paddock sagged slightly where it hadn't before. A section of grass scorched pale where machinery had idled too long weeks earlier. A pile of cleared brush she'd meant to burn off properly when conditions were right.

Later, she'd told herself.

Later was becoming a habit she could feel the land resenting.

By midmorning, smoke rose faintly on the far horizon - distant, diffuse, nothing urgent. Someone else managing their country. Someone else choosing a window that felt safe enough.

Alice watched it longer than she needed to.

This was how fires began, she knew. Not with carelessness, but with confidence. With the belief that experience counted for more than conditions.

She turned away and checked the pumps again, the gauges holding steady but low. Restraint had its own cost. Everything was tighter now - margins shaved down until there was no room for error.

At lunch, she sat on the verandah with a sandwich she barely ate, watching heat shimmer above the paddocks. The land looked deceptively calm, stretched out and waiting.

She thought of Tom then - of the way he used to walk these paddocks with her, noticing what she missed, carrying half the mental load without needing to say so.

Absence, she was learning, wasn't loud. It was cumulative.

In the afternoon, Maggie Rowley stopped by.

"I won't stay," Maggie said, standing by the gate. "Just wanted you to know - they've lifted the fire danger rating tomorrow."

Alice nodded. "I saw."

"Some people are nervous," Maggie added. "About you being here alone."

"I'm not alone," Alice replied. "I'm responsible."

Maggie studied her for a moment, then nodded. "That's what I figured."

As Maggie drove away, the wind shifted - not stronger, just different. It carried the dry smell of the land more sharply now, lifting fine dust from the track and scattering it across the paddocks.

Alice stood still, letting it move past her, committing the feel of it to memory.

That night, she walked the perimeter again, torch cutting a narrow path through the dark. Everything looked fine. Everything always did, until it didn't.

When she finally went inside, she left the windows open despite the heat, listening to the night sounds - insects louder than usual, restless, insistent.

She lay awake long after midnight, the stillness pressing in around her.

Dry country, she thought, wasn't loud about its warnings. It whispered them.

And if you didn't listen closely enough, it stopped whispering altogether.

CHAPTER TWENTY-ONE

The wind arrived before the heat broke.

Alice noticed it first in the sound - the way the trees shifted from a low rustle to something sharper, more insistent. Leaves scraped against one another instead of whispering. Loose tin rattled once, then settled, then rattled again.

She stood on the verandah with a mug gone cold in her hands and watched the paddocks respond.

Grass leaned. Dust lifted. The land adjusted its posture.

This wasn't unusual. Wind was part of the country's language. But today it felt purposeful, as if it had chosen a direction and committed to it.

She checked the forecast again. Fire danger elevated. Wind change late afternoon.

Late afternoon, she thought, meant nothing. Out here it could come early. Or not at all. Or arrive sideways and stay.

Alice spent the morning doing the things you did when you told yourself you were being sensible. She cleared a narrow strip along the fence line she'd meant to get to earlier. She shifted the brush pile further from the shed. She checked extinguishers she hoped she wouldn't need.

Each task finished with the same unease.

Enough, but only just.

By midday, the wind had warmed. It no longer cooled the skin - it dried it. The smell of the place changed with it, green notes stripped away until all that remained was dust, sap, and the faint tang of old smoke that never quite left country like this.

A ute slowed on the road and stopped at the gate.

Jack Rowley climbed out, hat pulled low, eyes already scanning the paddocks.

"Thought I'd check in," he said.

Alice nodded. "You're not the only one."

"Wind's got people twitchy," Jack said. "They're cancelling burns. Postponing work."

She followed his gaze to the far ridge, where a faint haze sat low and unmoving. "Some didn't get the memo."

Jack's mouth tightened. "That's what worries me."

They stood there for a moment, listening.

"You've got help if you need it," Jack said. "Whatever people think - when it comes to fire, that stuff goes quiet."

"I know," Alice replied. And she did. Fire had a way of rearranging priorities.

Jack lingered, then nodded once and drove on.

The afternoon stretched. The sky bleached itself of colour until everything looked flatter, closer. Shadows sharpened. The wind shifted again - just a few degrees - but Alice felt it immediately, the way you felt a change in pressure before a storm.

This one wouldn't bring rain.

She walked the boundary one more time, boots kicking up dust where there should have been none.

The brush pile sat where she'd moved it, safe enough. The fence line held. The shed stood quiet.

Everything was fine.

That was the most dangerous part.

Near dusk, the wind strengthened suddenly, a clean, decisive push that bent the tops of the trees and carried sound with it. Somewhere far off, a dog barked once, then stopped.

Alice stood very still.

She closed her eyes and let the wind move over her, measuring it the way you did when instinct mattered more than data. Hot. Dry. Directional.

She felt it then - not fear, not certainty - but readiness snapping into place.

If something started today, it wouldn't creep.

It would run.

Alice turned back toward the house, already shifting into a different kind of attention. Doors closed. Gear moved closer. The quiet organisation of someone who knew that waiting was no longer an option.

As the light drained from the sky, the wind did not ease.

It held.

And the land, stripped of softness, waited with it.

CHAPTER TWENTY-TWO

The fire didn't announce itself.

It arrived the way most real things did - sideways, almost apologetically, as if it hadn't yet decided whether it intended to stay.

Alice was in the shed when she smelled it.

Not smoke - not yet - but heat carried on the wrong wind. The air thickened suddenly, pressing against her skin with a weight she recognised instinctively. She straightened, tools falling forgotten to the bench, and listened.

At first there was nothing.

Then a sound reached her - faint, irregular, like something breathing badly.

She stepped outside.

A thin line of smoke lifted from the fence line on the western boundary, pale and uncertain against the sky. It wavered, then flattened abruptly as the wind pushed it sideways, dragging it low and fast across the paddock.

Alice didn't hesitate.

She ran.

By the time she reached the fence, flame had already found something to hold. Dry grass caught eagerly, lifting and folding over itself with quiet efficiency. The fire wasn't tall. It wasn't dramatic.

It was purposeful.

She stamped at the edge with her boots, swinging the shovel she'd grabbed without thinking, beating the flames back where she could. For a moment - just a moment - it seemed to work.

Then the wind shifted.

Not a change so much as a decision.

The fire lifted, shed its restraint, and moved.

Alice staggered back as heat surged toward her, the air suddenly alive, crackling with urgency. The flames ran the grass like a fuse, leaping forward in fast, greedy lines that ignored the boundary she'd trusted.

"No," she said aloud, the word useless and human and far too small.

She turned and ran for the ute, heart hammering, mind already jumping ahead - stock first, always. She grabbed the radio, her phone, keys clutched tight in her fist.

"Fire at Taravale," she said into the radio, voice clipped and steady despite the way her hands shook. "Western boundary. Wind-driven."

She didn't wait for the reply.

By the time she reached the yards, smoke had thickened, flattening the sky into something close and oppressive. The fire wasn't roaring yet - not fully - but it was moving with intent, advancing faster than she liked, faster than she could outrun if she misjudged it.

She opened gates, drove stock hard toward the safer paddock, coughing as smoke clawed at her throat. The animals moved reluctantly at first, confused, then quicker as instinct caught up with hesitation.

Good, she thought grimly. Let fear do its job.

Ash began to fall, light as snow, settling into her hair, her clothes, the hollows of her skin. The heat pressed closer now, breathing down the back of her neck.

Alice moved automatically, actions stacked neatly on training and memory. There was no room for panic - only sequence.

When she finally looked back toward the boundary, the fire had crossed it.

Taravale was no longer on the outside.

She stood for a split second longer than she should have, the enormity of it settling like a physical blow.

This wasn't a punishment. This wasn't a message.

This was the land doing what it did when conditions aligned and restraint failed.

Alice turned back toward the work, jaw set, lungs burning, and pushed forward.

Later - much later - she would remember the exact moment the fire stopped being containable and became something else entirely.

But for now, there was only movement, heat, and the knowledge that whatever the land had kept until now, it had decided to take its share.

CHAPTER TWENTY-THREE

By the time the first ute arrived, the fire had found its stride.

It moved low and fast, riding the wind the way it had been waiting to. Flames bent sideways, skimming the ground, devouring grass in clean, efficient lines. Smoke flattened the sky until everything felt closer, tighter, louder.

Alice didn't look back.

She moved with the fire now, not against it - opening gates, pushing stock hard toward the safer paddock, trusting instinct over hope. The animals surged forward, panic finally doing what training couldn't.

Good, she thought. Keep moving.

A ute skidded to a stop near the yards. Jack Rowley jumped out before it had fully braked, already pulling on gloves.

"Where do you need us?" he shouted.

Alice pointed without hesitation. "Southern boundary. Hold it if you can. Don't chase it."

Jack nodded once and ran.

More vehicles followed - neighbours, volunteers, the familiar red and white of the local brigade cresting the rise like something solid in a world suddenly untrustworthy. Radios crackled. Voices layered over one another, clipped and professional.

Someone handed Alice a helmet. She took it, jammed it on, didn't thank them.

This wasn't chaos.

It was sequence.

The fire pushed hard along the western paddock, then lifted suddenly, spotting ahead as embers leapt the line Alice had hoped would hold. She watched it happen and made the call before anyone else could argue.

"Let that paddock go," she said into the radio. "Protect the house. Protect the yards."

There was a beat of silence.

Then: "Copy."

The old shed went next.

Alice saw it catch from the corner of her eye - flame licking up the dry timber like it had always known where to start. For a moment, something sharp and personal twisted in her chest.

Then she let it burn.

That shed held more history than safety now. Old tools. Old habits. Old silences.

She turned away and kept moving.

Heat pressed close, the air alive with noise - crackle, roar, the thud of helicopters overhead. Ash coated her teeth, her skin, the inside of her mouth. Time lost its usual shape.

Somewhere in the middle of it, Alice realised something strange.

She wasn't afraid.

She was busy.

When the wind finally shifted - not kinder, just different - the fire slowed enough to be met head-on. Crews dug in. Water fell where it mattered. The line steadied, then held.

By the time night closed in, Taravale was scarred but standing.

Alice stood at the edge of the blackened paddock, helmet tucked under her arm, watching the last tongues of flame die down into glowing lines beneath the dark.

Someone touched her shoulder. "You did well," a voice said.

She nodded, not trusting herself to speak.

The fire hadn't taken everything.

But it had taken what it came for.

CHAPTER TWENTY-FOUR

Morning came grey and quiet.

The smoke had thinned, lifting just enough to let the damage show without softening it. Alice walked the property alone, boots sinking into ash that still held warmth beneath the surface.

The western paddock was gone.

Not damaged - erased. Black ground stretched out where grass had fed stock and memory for years. Fence posts leaned at odd angles, wire twisted and slack.

She stood there longer than she meant to, letting the loss register properly.

This was the price of wind and heat and timing.

The shed was a skeleton.

Tin peeled back, beams collapsed inward, the shape of it barely recognisable. Among the wreckage lay fragments of things that had once mattered - tools inherited and never used, boxes she hadn't opened in years, remnants of a past that had insisted on staying quiet.

Ash, she thought. Just ash now.

The house still stood.

Soot-streaked. Smoke-scarred. But intact. Windows blackened but unbroken. The verandah rail warm beneath her hand.

She let out a breath she hadn't realised she was holding.

Stock losses were minimal. Fewer than she'd feared. Enough to hurt, not enough to break her.

Alice marked it all down in her head without writing anything yet. Losses needed to be named before they could be managed.

Neighbours came and went quietly through the morning. No speeches. No reassurances that rang hollow. Just nods, water bottles pressed into her hands, someone leaving a tray of sandwiches on the bonnet of her ute without comment.

Jack Rowley lingered last.

"Could've been worse," he said.

"Yes," Alice replied. "And it wasn't an accident."

Jack studied the blackened paddock. "You made the right calls."

She nodded. "I did."

He hesitated, then said, "Some things needed burning."

Alice looked at him sharply.

He shrugged. "Doesn't make it easy."

"No," she agreed. "But it makes it clean."

When he left, Alice stood alone again, the property quiet in a way that felt earned rather than empty.

She thought of Tom then - not with longing, but with understanding. He would have seen this clearly. The necessity of it. The way loss rearranged what mattered.

But he wasn't here.

And she didn't reach for her phone.

As the sun finally burned through the haze, light fell across the blackened ground and the untouched paddocks beyond it.

Contrast, she thought. Truth did that too.

The fire hadn't taken Taravale from her.

It had stripped it back.

And standing there, ash on her boots and smoke in her hair, Alice understood what the land had left behind:

Not devastation. Not victory.

Just what could stand honestly in the open.

CHAPTER TWENTY-FIVE

Dawn came without ceremony.

The sky lightened gradually, colour seeping back into the world as if testing whether it was welcome. Alice stood on the verandah and watched it happen, the mug in her hands untouched, the smell of smoke still threaded through the air.

The land looked altered in the daylight.

Not ruined. Changed.

Blackened ground lay open where the paddock had been, stark and honest. Beyond it, green still held where the fire hadn't reached, the line between them sharp enough to hurt your eyes.

Alice took a breath and stepped down into the day.

She walked the boundary slowly, deliberately, letting herself see what remained instead of cataloguing what was gone. Fence posts still stood where they'd mattered most. Gates swung freely. The creek still ran - lower, quieter, but there.

Life, she thought. Reduced, but intact.

Near the yards, volunteers moved quietly, packing hoses, coiling lines. There was no chatter now, no nervous humour. Just the steady efficiency of people who knew when the work was done.

Someone nodded to her. Someone else touched her arm briefly in passing. No one asked questions that didn't need answers.

This was the respect that came after.

By mid-morning, the last of the trucks pulled away. Dust settled back into the drive. The property grew still again, the silence deeper now for having been earned.

Alice stood alone near the blackened paddock and let the quiet settle around her.

She felt it then - not relief, not grief - but something steadier. A sense of alignment she hadn't known she'd been missing.

The fire had taken what it could.

It hadn't taken her.

She knelt and pressed her palm to the ash-warm ground, feeling the heat still trapped beneath the surface. Somewhere under that blackness, seeds waited. The land didn't rush these things.

Neither would she.

Later, she returned to the house and washed the smoke from her hands. Soot swirled briefly down the sink before disappearing entirely. The ordinary act grounded her more than she expected.

She noticed then what else remained.

The house still held its shape. The table still bore the marks of meals eaten and plans made. The envelope Tom had left sat untouched where she'd placed it days ago.

She didn't open it yet.

Absence pressed at her, sharp but clean. Not a wound anymore - a space. Something she could move around without pretending it wasn't there.

Alice stepped back outside as the sun climbed higher, heat already beginning to gather again. The land stretched before her, scarred but standing, asking nothing she couldn't give.

This, she realised, was what endurance actually looked like.

Not holding on to everything. Not pretending nothing had changed.

But standing in the open, seeing clearly what was left, and choosing to keep going anyway.

She turned back toward the house, already thinking in sequences again - repairs, rotations, the slow work of restoration. Not urgent. Not heroic.

Necessary.

And as she crossed the threshold, Alice understood something with quiet certainty:

The fire had taken its share.

The land had kept its truth.

And what it had left her with was enough.

CHAPTER TWENTY-SIX

The fire left behind a kind of silence Alice had never heard before.

Not the absence of sound - there was still wind, the occasional crack of cooling timber, the distant low of stock unsettled by smoke - but a silence stripped of expectation. Nothing waited. Nothing asked.

She stood at the edge of the paddock long after the trucks had gone, boots sinking into ash that was still warm beneath the surface. The ground held heat the way it held memory - slowly, stubbornly.

The fence line was gone in places. Posts reduced to blackened stubs. Wire slack and twisted like it had tried to flee and failed.

Alice noted it all without urgency.

Urgency had burned itself out hours earlier.

Someone had draped a jacket over her shoulders at some point. She wasn't sure who. She became aware of it only when the weight began to irritate her, the fabric catching at her neck.

She shrugged it off and laid it over the gate.

The sky had cleared to a hard, indifferent blue. Smoke thinned into something that looked almost harmless, drifting away like it hadn't been the same thing that tore through the paddocks hours earlier.

Jack Rowley stood nearby, arms folded, watching the same stretch of land.

"You should go inside," he said.

"In a minute."

Jack nodded. He didn't argue. He understood the need to stay with the damage until it stopped changing.

"I'll be back at first light," he said. "We'll walk it properly then."

Alice nodded. "Thank you."

He hesitated. "You did everything right."

Alice looked at him. "It still burned."

Jack met her gaze evenly. "Fire doesn't ask permission."

When he left, the quiet closed in again.

Alice walked back toward the house slowly, counting her steps without meaning to. The verandah boards creaked under her boots. The screen door complained softly as she pushed it open.

Inside, the house smelled wrong.

Not smoke exactly - that would have made sense - but a faint, acrid residue that clung to the air, settling into fabric and timber. The smell of something changed permanently.

She closed the door behind her and stood there, hands hanging uselessly at her sides.

The kitchen table was still bare.

She'd cleared it before the fire, stacking papers, putting things away like order might keep the land calm. The instinct embarrassed her now, though she understood it.

She filled a glass with water and drank half of it too fast, coughing as it went down. Her hands were shaking properly now, the delayed reaction arriving with no interest in dignity.

Alice set the glass down and pressed her palms flat against the bench until the trembling eased.

She checked the house room by room.

Nothing burned. Nothing broken. Everything intact.

The ordinariness of it made her chest ache.

When she finally sat on the edge of the bed, the exhaustion hit her all at once - heavy, disorienting, like being pulled under. She lay back without removing her boots, eyes open, staring at the ceiling as the events replayed themselves in fragments.

Wind. Heat. The sound of something giving way. A shouted instruction she couldn't place.

She turned her head into the pillow and breathed slowly until the images dulled.

Sleep came in shallow pieces.

She woke once, convinced she smelled smoke again and sat bolt upright, heart hammering, before the logic caught up. Another time she woke because the house was too quiet, the silence pressing in around her like a held breath.

At some point before dawn, she woke with the certainty that she had forgotten something.

The feeling sat in her chest - vague, insistent.

She lay there, searching her body for the answer, then realised what it was.

She hadn't checked the back fence.

Not properly. Not after.

It wasn't urgent. It wasn't even important in the scheme of things.

But it was hers.

Alice swung her legs off the bed and pulled on a jumper, the fabric rough against her skin. Outside, the air was cool, the night finally releasing its grip on the heat.

She walked down the slope with a torch, beam cutting a narrow tunnel through the dark.

The fence was damaged but standing. A section sagged where wire had snapped. Manageable. Fixable.

She rested her hand on the post and let herself breathe.

It was then - absurdly - that the urge to call Tom arrived.

Not earlier, in the chaos. Not during the long hours of work. Now.

She could picture him too easily: the way he'd listen without interrupting, the steadiness of him like ballast. The way he'd come if she asked, no questions, no conditions.

The comfort of it tempted her.

She took her phone from her pocket and stared at the screen, thumb hovering.

She imagined his voice on the line - concern held carefully in check, trust offered without pressure.

If she called him now, she wouldn't have to be strong for a few minutes.

That was the danger of it.

Alice lowered the phone again.

She didn't need saving. And she wouldn't let him pay for something she'd chosen to carry.

She slid the phone back into her pocket and leaned her forehead briefly against the fence post, eyes closed.

"I'm alright," she said quietly, though no one was there to hear it.

When she returned to the house, dawn was beginning to lift the edge of the sky. Pale light crept into the kitchen, revealing ash tracked across the floor, the faint outline of her boots where she'd walked in and out without noticing.

She left it.

Some things didn't need to be erased immediately.

She made tea this time and drank it slowly, the warmth settling into her chest. Her body ached now, properly, the honest ache of effort and aftermath.

By the time the sun cleared the ridge, Alice was back outside, walking the boundary again, notebook in hand. She wrote without overthinking - lengths, losses, priorities.

Work restored order.

From the rise, she could see the full scar of the fire - the way it had torn through one section and spared another without logic or apology. The land didn't explain itself.

It never had.

As she stood there, the truth of it settled into place with unexpected calm.

This was what came after.

Not resolution. Not relief.

Just continuation - altered, marked, still moving forward.

Alice closed the notebook and tucked it under her arm.

She didn't look back at the house as she walked toward the next task.

There would be time for that later.

For now, there was land to tend, fences to fix, and a life that required her presence - not her permission.

And though she carried the absence of Tom like a bruise she refused to press, she understood, finally, that staying did not always mean holding on.

Sometimes, it meant standing alone.

CHAPTER TWENTY-SEVEN

Tom didn't come back.

Alice hadn't expected him to - not really - but the absence still registered like a sound you noticed only after it stopped. The fire had given her a reason to believe he might appear on the horizon, boots on, ready to work without explanation.

He didn't.

Instead, help arrived sideways.

A load of fencing wire delivered before dawn. A generator she hadn't ordered dropped at the gate with a note taped to the side. A number sent her a text with the name of a contractor who didn't ask questions.

Alice recognised the pattern immediately.

This was Tom.

Present without being seen.

She hated how much it worked.

She walked the boundary that afternoon with the map folded under her arm, marking what needed rebuilding, what could wait, what would never be put back the way it had been. Every so often, she caught herself framing a thought the way she used to when he was beside her.

Tom would say-

She stopped herself.

Not because it hurt.

Because it didn't help.

Late in the day, Maggie Rowley drove up and leaned against the fence beside her.

"He's keeping his distance," Maggie said.

"Yes."

"On purpose."

"Yes."

Maggie studied her face. "He's not punishing you."

"I know."

"He's making it possible for you to keep standing where you are."

Alice nodded. "That's what makes it harder."

They stood together, the paddock stretching out in front of them, black and quiet and waiting.

"He asked me how you were," Maggie added.

Alice looked at her. "And?"

"I said you were keeping busy."

Alice smiled faintly. "I am."

That night, Alice sat at the kitchen table with the window open, the cool air moving gently through the house. She spread out the papers from the envelope Tom had left, reading them again, slower this time.

She understood now why he hadn't stayed.

Not because he was afraid of what they'd find.

Because he knew what it would cost her to carry it.

She folded the documents carefully and placed them back where they belonged.

Outside, a vehicle passed on the road and didn't slow.

Alice watched the taillights disappear and felt the echo of the leaving settle fully into place.

This wasn't abandonment.

This was love choosing distance over damage.

She closed the folder and rested her hands flat on the table, grounding herself in the ordinary.

Tomorrow, there would be meetings. Conversations. Decisions that would ripple outward whether she wanted them to or not.

But tonight, she allowed herself one small, private truth.

She missed him.

And missing him didn't weaken her resolve.

It clarified it.

Alice turned off the light and went to bed alone, the house quiet around her, the land outside holding what it always had - memory, consequence, and the long echo of choices made.

CHAPTER TWENTY-EIGHT

The land didn't rush its recovery.

Alice noticed it first in the mornings - the way the ash cooled more slowly than she expected, the way the blackened paddock held the night longer, releasing its warmth only when the sun climbed high enough to insist.

She learned the new shape of Taravale by walking it.

Every day, she walked a little further into what had burned, letting her eyes adjust to the starkness. There was no denying the loss now. No softening it with optimism. The ground was bare and honest, stripped of the cover it had worn for years.

Still, it held.

Life had a way of waiting for permission.

The community settled into something quieter, too. Less talk. Fewer glances. The story had reached the point where it could no longer be fed by speculation alone. What remained were facts - and facts didn't travel as fast.

Alice spent her days repairing what mattered and leaving the rest untouched. Some fences would be rebuilt. Some would remain broken a while longer. The decisions felt simpler now, even when they weren't easy.

She stopped explaining herself.

Not out of defiance, but because explanation suggested uncertainty, and she no longer had any.

One afternoon, she knelt at the edge of the burned paddock and pressed her fingers into the soil. It was still dark beneath the surface, still warm in places, but when she dug a little deeper, she felt it - the faint resistance of moisture, the promise held just out of sight.

The land was not finished.

Neither was she.

Tom remained absent in the way she had come to recognise - deliberate, careful, protective. His help arrived through other hands now, woven so subtly into the fabric of things that she could accept it without being pulled backward by it.

She didn't thank him.

He would have understood why.

The documents from the envelope no longer sat untouched. Alice had begun the work they demanded - slowly, methodically, without spectacle. Names would be spoken when it was time. The truth would move forward at the pace it required, not the pace that made anyone comfortable.

At night, she slept deeply.

Not because the ache was gone, but because she was no longer fighting it.

On the final evening before the season tipped fully into summer, Alice stood on the verandah and watched the light fade from the hills. The air was clear now. The smell of smoke had lifted entirely, replaced by dust and eucalyptus and the faint green scent of things trying again.

She thought about everything the land had kept from her.

And everything it had taken.

And finally, what it had left behind.

Not answers. Not forgiveness. Not reunion.

Just truth, carried in the open. Just ground that would grow again in its own time. Just herself - standing, unhidden, and no longer afraid of what came next.

Alice turned back inside and closed the door against the cooling night.

Behind her, Taravale lay quiet and scarred and alive.

And whatever the land would reveal one day, whatever it might return or refuse to return, she would meet it the same way she always had in the end.

With her eyes open.

EPILOGUE

The land did not look kinder after the fire. Just more honest.

Ash cooled quickly once the smoke cleared, leaving the paddocks stripped back to line and contour. Black ground gave way, slowly, to thin green threads that pushed up without ceremony or promise. Recovery, Alice had learned, was not an apology. It was simply a response.

Summer settled in.

The house held the heat well. Windows stayed open. Dust gathered where it always had. The marks of smoke remained faintly along the eaves - not damage, exactly. Evidence.

Alice did not scrub them away.

Work returned to its ordinary rhythm. Fences were rebuilt where they mattered. Others were left to wait. The land adjusted, as it always did, to the care it was given and the care it was denied.

What did not return was quiet.

Letters arrived with careful language and unfamiliar names. Interest, framed politely. Questions that reached beyond Taravale and did not bother pretending otherwise. Alice answered what she needed to and ignored what she didn't.

Tom remained absent.

Not gone - never that - but deliberately out of view. His help came through other hands now, routed cleanly, never drawing attention to itself. Alice understood the discipline of that choice. Some truths travelled better without witnesses attached.

One evening, she stood at the edge of the burned paddock as the light faded, watching the land settle into night. The boundary between blackened ground and unburned grass was still sharp. It would soften with time.

Everything did.

The creek kept running. The gumtrees stood. The house waited for nothing.

Alice turned back toward the work of the next day with a steadiness she had earned, no longer sheltered by silence or softened by hope.

The land had not taken sides.

It had simply stopped keeping what was never meant to stay hidden.

What the Land Reveals comes next.

ABOUT THE AUTHOR

Emily Fraser writes rural romantic suspense set in Australia, where landscape is not a backdrop but a force, and where silence, loyalty, and human connection shape the story as powerfully as plot.

Her Taravale Series explores land, memory, consequence, and the cost of truth in small communities - stories where love is tested not by absence of feeling, but by the choices people make when staying quiet would be easier.

What the Land Keeps introduced readers to Taravale.

What the Land Leaves continues that story, shifting from inheritance to consequence.

Emily lives and works on the land she writes about, where stories are shaped by weather, work, and the long memory of place.